# YOUR VAMPIRE'S THRALL

## LACEY BUCKLES

*Lacey Buckles*
*xox*

This is a work of fiction. Names, characters, places, and incidents either are the product of the author's imagination or are used fictitiously. Any resemblance to actual persons, living or dead, events, or locales is entirely coincidental.

Copyright 2025 © Lacey Buckles

All rights reserved. No part of this book may be reproduced or used in any manner without written permission of the copyright owner except for the use of quotations in a book review.

ISBN 978-1-913673-25-3

*For every dirty daydreamer reading this — whether you imagine yourself on your knees, or imagine someone else on theirs. You're exactly where you belong.*

# CONTENT WARNING

This book is a dark, paranormal romance with sharp teeth and sharper edges. It contains explicit sexual content, violence, blood, and themes of control and surrender that will not be to everyone's taste. Please check the warnings below carefully before diving in.

- Explicit sexual scenes (MF, MFM, anal play, light bondage, BDSM dynamics)
- Blood-drinking and feeding during sex
- Power imbalance, coercive undertones, and possessive domination
- Violence, including on-page murder
- Kidnapping, restraint, and psychological manipulation
- Horror elements (fear, gore, and supernatural dread)

As with all *Your Dark Desires* stories, this book is intended for mature audiences only. If these elements are not for you, please step away safely. If they are—welcome. This story is written to consume you.

# THE BOOKBINDER'S INVITATION

You've wandered too far from the light, little mortal.

I can smell your fear.

I can taste your curiosity.

And I know exactly how to bind them together until they are indistinguishable from desire.

Within these pages, you are prey—beautiful, trembling, and already caught.

Two predators circle you here: one cold as moonlight, the other hot as fresh blood. They will not fight over you. They will take you together.

Every kiss will be a claim.

Every touch will mark you.

Every bite will hollow you out until nothing remains but the story I choose to leave behind.

You are not my first. You will not be my last. Others have walked these same pages, thinking their story belonged only to them.

They were wrong.

You may close the book at any time. But we both know you won't.

Come. Let me write your surrender. And remember, desire is the story we dare not speak aloud...

Do you dare to become your vampire's thrall?

# CHAPTER ONE

Another podium. Another auditorium.

Another crowd of polite academics pretending they aren't bored out of their skulls.

I step away from the lectern to soft applause. Not rapturous, but respectful. That's the best I can hope for in a room like this—men in corduroy blazers pretending not to be threatened, women calculating whether my career trajectory reflects favour or folly.

They called my latest paper provocative. Forward-thinking. One reviewer even called it "bracingly speculative."

What they won't say—but all suspect—is that I meant it.

Because I do.

I've seen enough buried fragments, mistranslated footnotes, and conveniently lost documents to know the truth hides in plain sight. Vampires exist. I just haven't met one. Yet.

Two more speakers to endure. A handful of questions after. Then I'll vanish like I always do—flight booked for tomorrow, passport already tucked into my coat. Another city. Another dusty collection of indecipherable fragments. Another client hoping I can read what no one else dares touch.

It's not boredom. Not exactly. It's... containment.

Like I was built for something larger, and I've spent a decade shrinking myself to fit the walls of institutions.

Finally, the event draws to a close and I make my way from the stage.

The last of the handshakes are fading. My colleagues are either heading to the wine reception or pretending not to rush toward taxis. I slip out through the foyer, heels clicking on smooth tile, coat draped over one arm, already half-thinking about the hotel bar. Dusk is pulling shadows across the ground like a blanket.

A quick cab ride to my hotel and the stool at the bar with my name on it. The bar is bustling with early-evening drinkers, people fresh from meetings and conferences. I head straight for a vacant stool next to a handsome young man leaning against the bar—alone, unreadable, eyes on his phone. Not drinking. Not waiting. Just... still.

There's something predatory in the stillness. Not aggressive, refined. Like a creature that's never needed to chase what it wants.

He looks up as I draw closer, movements fluid, unhurried. The phone disappears into his coat pocket like it was never there.

"Dr Cavendish."

I stop short, one hand brushing the back of the bar stool. Not startled. But alert.

There's a charge in the air now, faint but undeniable.

"Do I know you?"

"No. But I'm familiar with your work. I enjoyed your recent paper. Very insightful."

"Thank you." I've heard it before, especially from handsome men. And he most definitely is that. Dark, slicked back hair, a strong jaw, pale skin and bright, blue eyes. My guard is up. As usual. I slide up onto the high stool and order a dry Martini.

The man smiles, just a little, a dimple appearing in his cheek.

"My name is Darius Draper. I represent a client who also enjoyed your paper and would like to hire you to consult on some artefacts."

I glance at him sideways. "Let me guess. He wants to show me proof." I've heard that before too and most of the time it turns out to be nothing. I'm just as sceptical now as ever.

"Well, that's what he'd like you to determine. He has something in his possession—a collection of documents requiring your specific expertise."

"What sort of documents?"

"Unusual ones."

Of course.

"What exactly are you offering me, Mr Draper?"

"A fully funded contract. Discretion guaranteed. The work will begin immediately. There's a private flight for you tonight to Edinburgh. We're prepared to meet your standard consulting rate. In fact..." He leans in slightly. "We'll exceed it."

He reaches around to the bar and slides a thick envelope along it towards me.

"This is a sample of the items we'd like you to analyse."

The plain envelope is about an inch thick. There are no markings on it besides my name and hotel handwritten on it. Inside is a stack of photos and I flip through them. They showcase a collection of ancient-looking documents written in Sumerian, by the looks of it. A slip of black paper is included and on it, in neat, white print, is a note addressed to me.

*Dear Dr Cavendish,*

*Please find enclosed a sample of the work we'd like you do undertake. I apologise for not sending the originals, they are too delicate to be moved but await your attention here in Edinburgh. I trust that this will ease any doubts of the seriousness of my offer, or the authenticity of the artefacts. I believe you will find this project most stimulating.*

*Regards,*

*T.*

I turn the note over but there is nothing further. I examine the photos more closely. I can't deny a little curiosity. I'd like to know what's really on the table here. The script on the photographed documents is definitely Sumerian—but there's something wrong about it. Stylised, almost ceremonial. Not standard temple texts or merchant ledgers. Ritualistic, maybe. A fragment of something liturgical, or older than that. Older than anything I've translated in years.

I slide the photographs back into the wallet but keep the note out, smoothing the black paper flat beside my untouched drink.

Darius moves a touch closer, his body mere inches from mine. He dips his head level with mine and a soft, warm whisper caresses my ear.

"We can show you proof, Dr Cavendish. Exactly the kind you've been looking for. Not in ancient documents, in the flesh."

I jerk my head back and fix my cool gaze on his face. Is he really offering me what I think?

"There's a car waiting for us right now. If you're interested, collect your things and meet me in the lobby in fifteen minutes."

Just like that, he's gone. He moves too quickly for me to see and I'm left holding my breath and searching the bar behind me for a sign of him, but there is none. I glance around and no one else seems to have noticed. The thick envelope still sits on the bar in front of me. It was definitely real. Not some exhaustion-induced hallucination.

I abandon my Martini and rush up to my room to pack. I have a plane to catch.

Darius Draper is true to his word. He's waiting for me in the hotel lobby, dressed in the same fine suit and long, black coat as before. He holds out a hand, gesturing for me to exit the building ahead of him while he holds open the glass door. A black car with a driver behind the wheel waits at the kerb and we slide into it. I keep my carry-on at my feet. I wouldn't normally get into a car with a stranger and the hairs standing up on the back of my neck tell me I'm right to be cautious. I have pepper spray in my handbag.

The drive to the small airport out of town passes quickly with very little conversation. Before I know it, I'm boarding a private jet with Darius Draper and leaving my own country for a foreign city steeped in history.

It's madness. But so was chasing phantoms through forgotten languages for ten years. At least this one has a face—and a jet.

I sleep a little on the flight, but there's too much adrenaline in my system to really let me rest.

We arrive in the early morning and as Darius and I descend the steps onto the tarmac, he pulls a hood up over his head, even though it's not raining. Another car much like the first one waits for us right there by the plane and again I'm steered into it and shuttled away to God knows where.

Darius's demeanour doesn't exactly invite conversation. But I do notice that he has no luggage.

I steal glances at him on the drive. His hood is back behind his neck, his hair slightly tousled. His jaw is defined, his skin smooth and pale and those eyes—so bright. He catches me staring at him and cracks a small smile, revealing that dimple again.

"Sorry," I whisper, looking away.

"It's quite all right."

As we move through the winding streets, the city unfolds in layers beyond the tinted windows. Not glossy, not showy—just old, like it's been waiting too long to tell me something important. Shadows lean long across sandstone buildings, their façades aged to gold in the first rays of morning sunlight. Church spires claw the sky. The cobbled roads glisten faintly from earlier rain.

It feels like a city built on secrets.

"Where are we going?" I ask, though I already suspect I won't be told the full truth.

"You'll be staying in a private residence in the Old Town," Darius replies. "A short walk from the archive. Secure. Discreet."

We pass beneath an arched bridge flanked with blackened statues, and I catch a glimpse of the castle high above us, silhouetted against a bruised sky.

"How long have you lived here?" I ask.

"A long time."

It's non-committal enough to irritate me, but I don't push. He's not the one I came here for. Still, he fascinates me in a quiet way. The way people do when you can sense they've seen things you haven't, and won't ever say so out loud.

"You don't have a Scottish accent," I say, curious and trying to ignore the way my stomach just flipped.

"No, I'm not originally from Scotland." He glances at me and smiles. It's dazzling. He doesn't look old enough to have lived here for a long time, but to have been old enough when he arrived that he didn't pick up the accent. He can't be more than thirty.

My lips quirk at the corner and I unashamedly gaze at his handsome features.

The car slips through one more tight turn and comes to a stop in a quiet square nestled between two towering rows of Georgian buildings. Ivy climbs the old stonework like veins. Lights glow behind mullioned windows. It's beautiful in that particularly Scottish way—weathered, elegant, and faintly melancholic.

In a flurry of too-quick movement, Darius is out of the car and holding open my door, gesturing toward a black door set into a small recess.

"This will be your residence for the duration of your work. You'll find everything prepared inside. Groceries. Communications. A workspace."

"And the archive?"

"You'll be escorted there tonight. For now, rest. Acclimate. Read, if you like." He hands me two sleek brass keys. No fob, no label. Just a simple weight in my hand. "Your host will be in touch soon."

"And who is that, exactly?" I ask, just to see what he'll say.

Darius smiles. This time, it's the kind that suggests he knows far more than he's willing to share.

"You'll know him when you meet him."

The first key opens the black door and Darius

escorts me up a steep flight of stairs immediately inside it. The other key in my hand unlocks the single door at the top. Inside, the town house smells of wood polish.

"If you need anything, there's a number in the welcome folder. I'm available at all hours."

"Of course you are," I murmur.

He inclines his head, offers one last fleeting not-quite-smile, and is gone.

I close the door behind him and slide the chain into place. The silence that follows is immediate and oddly complete, as though the flat itself exhales once it's only me.

The space is beautiful. Thoughtfully curated, like someone anticipated the kind of comfort I prefer. High ceilings with moulded plasterwork, tall windows dressed in thick velvet drapes, and floors worn smooth by generations of footfall. A handsome fireplace with an electric fire set into it where once there would have been a real hearth. Bookshelves half-filled—some with local histories, others with more esoteric fare.

Modern conveniences are tucked into the edges. A sleek espresso machine sits on the marble counter in the kitchen. The desk in the corner has wireless charging built into the surface. My favourite tea blend waits in a ceramic jar beside a silver kettle. I didn't ask for this. Which means someone's been paying attention to me.

The flat is warm, lit by soft amber lamps, but a draught snakes across the floorboards near one of the living room windows as I pull back the curtains and look down into the square. The street is quiet. Empty.

It feels like a stage set, waiting for the play to begin.

I turn away. I want a shower. A change of clothes. A strong coffee. It's been a long night of travel.

After I unpack my things and take a shower, I settle on the king-sized bed fitted with cream and warm, sand-coloured bedding, and look around the room properly. On the bedside table is a strange package. Something wrapped in deep blue velvet cloth. When I pull the cloth back, it reveals a leather-bound book with no title. The cover is smooth, but not blank; there's a pattern in faded gold leaf covering the front.

I turn it over in my hands. No identifying marks. No author. Just that quiet, deliberate presence some old objects seem to carry—as though they've been touched too many times by too many people who wanted something.

I open the cover. There's no copyright page, no contents. Just two blank pages of thin paper that rustle as I carefully turn them. When I get to the text, the print is fine and the words feel instantly as if they were written just for me.

*Ah, you found me. Like the others who came before you. But don't be jealous, my darling. I shall whisper my invitation just for you. Come with me and let's discover your story together, Katrina.*

I close the book and look around the room. What the—? I open it again and scan the first page once more. It's definitely there, in print. My own name. I was already intrigued, but now? Now I'm enthralled.

## CHAPTER TWO

A bar isn't exactly the obvious location for a historical archive. But I roll with it. I step out of another black car, like the one that carried me from the airport. The driver is an unknown figure beyond dark glass. I step out of the car and approach the bar.

The windows are darkened and the street outside is quiet. No sign. No name. Just a single glass door with a brass handle. I pull on it and a gush of warm air spills out along with a wave of soft music and bubbling conversation and the scents of liquor and hot bodies.

I move inside and the door swings shut behind me. It's a stunning venue. Polished wood. Soft lighting. Ambient music humming low from hidden speakers. People cluster around tall tables, or on low sofas by the tinted windows. The buzz is welcoming and a nice change from the solitude of the apartment. But I have to admit to being confused about the location.

I move through the clustered tables to the bar

where a woman works the crowd, filling orders with grace and ease. She moves like someone used to order and control, dressed in a black shirt tucked neatly into dark jeans, auburn hair twisted into a severe knot.

Her eyes flick over me as she moves between orders. I get the impression I'm being weighed and filed, not welcomed. Another member of staff emerges from a door behind the bar and she hands off the work to him before making a direct line for me.

"Dr Cavendish?" She calls over the noise of the bar. I nod in reply. "I'm Lenora. I run *Thirst*." She extends a hand but there's frost in her tone. I reach out to shake her hand, surprised by the firmness of her grip.

"Great name for a bar," I say, trying to connect with this woman.

She merely shrugs. She gestures for me to follow and leads me behind the bar, through a discreet door. We head through a narrow passage to another door that looks like it ought to lead out of the back of the building. It opens with the soft hiss of hydraulics, revealing a narrow stairwell that descends into shadow.

"Watch your step. Some of the stones down there pre-date the club by centuries." Her Scottish accent is softer than her prickly tone.

I descend with a little hesitation. The stone steps are smooth and rounded. The air grows colder the deeper we go, the scent shifting from polished wood, liquor and citrus to something older. Paper, dust, and time. At the bottom, the stairs give way to a long corridor lined with arches and antique sconces—modern lighting hidden cleverly among them. And at the far end: a thick wooden door, sealed with a heavy bolt.

Lenora unlocks it with a key from her belt and pushes it open to reveal a room that steals my breath for half a second.

It's not large, but it's beautiful in its restraint. Stone walls lined with glass cases. A long oak table dominates the centre, surrounded by mismatched chairs that somehow work together. A brass reading lamp glows over a stack of already-prepared folders.

"Everything you need should be here. Supplies. Tools. Do not take anything from this room without clearance." Lenora bustles into the room, switching on lights.

"I wasn't planning to."

"Good."

She lingers for a moment longer than necessary.

"You'll meet him tonight." She pauses in the doorway. "He's been... looking forward to this." She turns on her heel and leaves without another word.

How mysterious. I still don't know anything about this client. I exhale and look around the space again.

I'm not sure what I expected.

But this?

I round the table and sit at the head by the stacks of folders and begin my work. I still don't really know exactly what's expected of me and part of me wonders if this job is something entirely new. I'm not really being asked to translate or interpret anything, more that I'm being invited to share some secret that I can't resist.

I pour over the texts. The collection is breathtaking. Some of the items are at least two thousand years old. The selection I'd been shown before arriving was all Sumerian, but there are items from all over the world here and I am beginning to see a pattern. There's no doubt of their authenticity. And each one refers or eludes to exactly what I've hypothesised and risked my entire career for. They're talking about the same thing, over and over. Hidden among myths, rites, and rituals, it's clear that throughout history, all over the world, people have recorded the existence of people with special characteristics. People who are stronger, faster and with more sensitive senses than regular humans. People with no pulse, people harmed by direct sunlight. *Vampires.*

I need a drink.

Not a quiet glass of wine at my desk or a soothing herbal tea. A real drink. Something strong enough to give me another reason for the room to be spinning—or at least take the edge off the realisation that I may have just spent the evening cataloguing undeniable evidence that vampires exist.

I climb the stairs from the archive, heels echoing a little too sharply on the old stone steps. My shoulders are tight. My thoughts even tighter.

The bar is as busy as when I arrived, full of business casual types, sipping espresso Martinis or cocktails that glint in the muted light. It's civilised. Sophisticated. Comfortingly ordinary.

Lenora stands behind the bar.

She doesn't greet me. Doesn't even blink. Just

watches as I approach, then turns her gaze deliberately toward the glass she's drying with an immaculate cloth.

I rest my hands on the bar and say, "Whisky. Neat. Please."

Without a word, she pours.

I take the glass and move to a stool at the far end, away from the customers. The light is dimmer here. The buzz of conversation more muted. I sit, the tumbler of aged Scotch heavy in my hand—until it isn't.

A tremor snakes through my fingers. Barely there, but enough. The rim of the glass slips against my palm. And I let out a soft, startled breath as the glass begins to fall.

Before I can even curse, it's caught.

A hand closes around it, smooth and unhurried, restoring it to the bar top without so much as a tremble.

Darius Draper settles into the seat beside me with casual ease. He doesn't look at the glass. He looks at me.

"Careful," he says, voice low and calm. "It's strong stuff."

I stare at him. At the hand that caught the glass. At the smooth-skinned face. At the eyes that seem just a little too bright for the light in the room.

I find my voice. "You're fast."

"Occupational hazard."

"Not human." It's not a question.

Darius smiles. Not smug. Not surprised. Just inevitable.

"I wondered how long it would take you."

Lenora glances our way then. Just for a second. No expression. No movement.

Then she turns her back.

"This is shock." Darius says, watching me. "You're not frightened."

I take the whisky and knock back half of it before answering.

"No," I say, setting the glass down gently this time. "Should I be?"

"Probably."

His honesty is refreshing and yet, as I glance sideways at him, the seriousness of his expression concerns me.

"Why have I really been brought here?"

"To translate the contents of the archive." He doesn't look at me, his gaze is fixed on the bottles lined up behind the bar.

I follow his gaze. The mirror behind the bottles reflects the deep mahogany, the lights, the bottles, me... but not the man sitting beside me. I return my gaze to him.

"I don't believe that. Are you my client?"

"No," he replies, sliding off the stool, his body pressing against mine. He leans one hand against the bar and dips his head to my ear. "Are you ready to meet him now?"

My breath is caught somewhere between my lungs and lips but before I can respond, Darius is guiding me gently from my stool. His movements are too quick. Surely someone else will notice. I glance around the softly humming bar and find not one eye looking this way. The patrons are far too concerned with themselves —or their phones—to notice anything else.

I've faced professors who hated my theories. I've stood in front of auditors tearing apart my research. I've spent ten years defending the idea that monsters once walked among us. But I never once asked myself what I'd do if I turned out to be right.

Darius leads me down a short corridor and over to a mirrored panel in the wall that slides aside at our approach. It's odd seeing only my own reflection and nothing of the man a step ahead of me.

The sliding mirror reveals an elevator lined with wooden panels and gold fixtures. I grasp the gold bar running around the walls and hold on as the lift descends.

Not back to the archive. Not to the documents or the relics or the safe bubble of academia.

This is something else entirely.

The doors glide open onto a different world.

Down one final corridor, past walls lined with obsidian tile and golden candle holders topped with black candles that burn with unnaturally red flames, the air shifts—warmer now, tinged with something metallic and decadent.

Then the sound hits me. Laughter. Music. The low thrum of a bass-line threaded with whispers.

We step past a red velvet curtain into a lounge carved from stone and shadow. Velvet drapes and chandeliers. Blood-red couches. Crystal glasses filled with something too dark to be wine.

They look like people. Beautiful, glittering, impossibly still. But they're not people. Not really. I feel it in my bones. They turn to watch me enter—not all at once, but like wolves would, each clocking the new arrival, assessing the scent of curiosity, the blood beneath the skin.

I keep walking. My gaze fixed on Darius's back as he leads me through the startlingly large crowd. I don't look away.

And then Darius steps aside, revealing the figure seated on a raised, crimson throne under a stone arch. Candles flicker on either side of him and a small gathering of beautiful creatures surround him, looking up at him like sycophants.

Tall. Immaculate. Shadow-draped and silver-eyed.

He doesn't smile.

He doesn't need to.

The others fade from my awareness.

The room might as well be empty.

Because I've just met the man—the monster—who's been pulling the strings all along.

And God help me... Some traitorous, trembling part of me wants to lean closer, not pull away.

His skin is almost translucent in the candlelight, his veins deep blue and purple beneath. His long, white hair hangs in perfect, thick sheets over his shoulders. He's dressed in an expensive, designer suit, tailored to his slender frame. He looks young and yet ancient at the same time and so beautiful I feel like I'll never see anything as captivating as long as I live. His face lights up as we approach and his silver eyes fix on me, and only me.

I'm only dimly aware of Darius dipping into a low bow and giving my name.

What's that pounding in my ears? Oh. My pulse. It flutters with my awareness of it and the sounds of the lounge begin to creep back into my perception.

"Dr Cavendish," he says as he rises to his feet. The people around him melt away, disappearing into the shadows. He extends a hand towards me, slowly, gracefully. The way he moves is utterly inhuman and breathtaking.

I take his offered hand but he doesn't shake it, he draws it up to his lips and, without breaking eye contact, brushes a soft kiss over my knuckles. Fuck. What on earth am I feeling?

"It is truly an honour to meet you at last. I apologise for not greeting you sooner." His voice is as smooth as silk and slices deep into my thoughts, past my racing heart, past the noise of the lounge, past my anxiety and inexplicable lust.

I find I can't respond. I'm hypnotised, caught in the trap laid for me.

He lowers my hand, but doesn't release it. His thumb caresses the skin on the back of my hand. His silver eyes remain fixed on mine and he steps closer, almost touching. I lift my chin to maintain eye contact. I couldn't look away even if I wanted to.

"You may call me Thorne."

"Katrina," I reply automatically. I'm momentarily surprised that I spoke and I blink several times. The rest of my surroundings flood back into my senses. Music flows beneath the hubbub of conversation and clinking of glasses. The lounge has low ceilings of sandstone and is lit by soft electric bulbs hanging on wires around the room, as well as by candles dotted around on low tables. There are nooks and crannies all around the room, packed with those deep, plush sofas and chairs, all deep crimson and rich plum. A long bar stands before the wall over by where we entered and with a painful swallow, I notice that alongside bottles of liquor are clear vats of thick, viscous blood. One of them drips. The sound lost among the noises in the lounge, but I swear I can hear each drop as it hits the small puddle beneath the tap.

"Welcome to Thirst, Katrina," Thorne says, his voice once again slicing smoothly through to me and tugging my attention back to his pale and glistening eyes. "I'm so glad you're here."

I don't respond immediately. My hand still tingles from where his lips touched it. I glance down. The sensation shouldn't linger—but it does.

"I've had... quite the welcome," I manage. "Your people are very—"

"Efficient?" he offers, one pale brow lifting.

"Guarded," I counter. "Except Darius. He's been welcoming."

Thorne laughs. Quietly. A sound like velvet unrolling. "He has a soft spot for the newly initiated. A rare trait."

I fold my arms, tilting my head. "Is that what I am?"

"Not yet." His eyes gleam. "But you're close. Closer than most who've walked through these doors. And closer still to what lies beneath."

I want to ask what that means, but he's already gesturing to a low, curved bench beside his throne. Not a command. An invitation.

I hesitate, then sit—perching, not lounging. A queen in a foreign court, still calculating the politics.

Thorne moves back to his seat and lowers himself gracefully into it. He doesn't fill the silence, and I realise with a jolt that it's deliberate. He's studying me. Not lecherously. Not even hungrily. Like a scholar presented with a rare manuscript.

"Your paper," he says finally. "Myth as Memory. A beautiful premise. That folklore is just a fragment of truth, wrapped in repetition. You almost had it."

My brows lift. "Almost?"

"You saw the pattern," he murmurs. "But not the hand behind it. You translated symbols. I lived them."

My pulse skips again. "And what? You've brought me here to correct my citations?"

That earns another laugh—richer this time. He leans forward, elbows resting lightly on his knees, fingertips pressed together.

"I brought you here because I admire your mind. Because unlike the others, you didn't flinch from what might be true. I wonder, Dr Cavendish... Katrina... how far would you go for the truth?" For a second, his eyes lose their sheen of civility. What remains is ancient. Merciless. If he wanted to kill me, he wouldn't need an excuse. A thought, a flick of his fingers, and I'd vanish like smoke. This is what I asked for, isn't it? Proof. Truth. And now I'm drowning in it. And then the look is gone.

That stops my racing thoughts.

"As far as it takes," I say carefully.

"Even if it costs you everything else?"

The air between us tightens, the sounds of the lounge receding again.

"It already has," I say quietly.

Something flickers in his eyes. Not pity. Not pride. Something like recognition.

"Good," he says. "Then we'll get along just fine."

There's another shift in the air. People seem to move closer and the music grows louder. I glance to my right and see two women locked in an embrace on a nearby sofa, but one of them is feeding on the other. Brazenly biting her pale neck while she writhes in ecstasy.

"You've had a long day," Thorne says, cutting into my transfixed state and dragging my attention back to him. "Darius will take you back to your flat. You may resume your work tomorrow."

"What is it, exactly, that you want me to do?"

"Oh, my apologies for not being more clear. I hope you'll forgive me." He presses a hand to his chest and dips his head in an almost courtly gesture of apology. I give him a nod. "I'd like you to translate the catalogue fully and compile a timeline of evidence. Not for publication, of course. We depend upon secrecy. But for my personal records."

"I see." And I do. I understand now. He brought me here to contain me. I'm not here to help uncover the truth. I'm here to make sure it stays buried—in velvet and stone and blood. I danced too close to the truth, to exposure. He can't have the world truly finding out about all of this. I swallow a hard lump in my throat as I wonder, perhaps belatedly, how far he'll go to keep his secrets.

# CHAPTER THREE

Before I'm even aware of having moved, Darius is at my side, a hand gently resting on the small of my back, guiding me back through the lounge. I glance back to see Thorne being swallowed by his flock. We step back into the elevator and the sounds of the underground lounge of Thirst fade away. My thoughts and awareness return to normal with some distance, and a considerable amount of stone, between myself and Thorne. I release a shaking breath and let out a small laugh. Darius twitches beside me and I glance up at him.

"Are you all right?" He frowns and places his hand on my shoulder.

"Yes. I'm all right. More or less."

"I haven't seen anyone resist him like that before."

"Sorry?" I ask, sobering slightly. The lift stops with only a slight bump and the doors glide silently open. But we don't step out of it. Darius is looking at me with a puzzled frown on his handsome features. "Resist what?"

"His..." Darius glances into the corridor before returning his gaze to me. "It's very difficult to look away from him, to talk back to him. You broke the hold he had on you."

"Did I?" I laugh nervously again and shake my head. "I wondered if he was putting some sort of mojo on me. It came and went."

"Well, that's odd." He turns and steps into the corridor, holding the doors open as I slowly follow him. The smile has died on my face again. So, Thorne has some sort of hypnotism? And I resisted it. Or maybe he released it. He seemed to want to have a conversation with me. If he's interested in my mind, why would he keep me under his spell?

We're walking briskly back through the public-facing bar but I'm hardly aware of it. Darius swings by the end of the bar and scoops up a paper bag from behind it before rejoining me and marching me towards the door. I step out through it into the cool street. The pavement is slick with rain and cars slosh past, their headlights glistening in the puddles. It's not raining now, though, and the dark sky is heavy with thick clouds. Darius reaches into the bag in his hand and pulls out something cylindrical wrapped in foil and passes it to me. The packet is warm and the scent of spiced chicken wafts up to me. I unwrap it and find a chicken wrap rolled tightly inside the foil.

Darius places a hand on my back again and guides me along the pavement in the direction of my flat, steering me around other pedestrians. I glance sideways at him. His sharp gaze scans the street constantly. There's an edge to him that I haven't seen before and a scowl etched onto his face.

I take a hesitant bite of the wrap. The flavours are an instant elixir to the tumult of emotions racing through me.

"I expect you have questions." Darius says at last.

"I do, but I'm still formulating them."

"You suspected the truth. That's why you were given this job. But I can see why seeing proof might still take some getting used to."

I let out a small snort of laughter. "Quite. Can you tell me anything about yourself?"

"I'm older than I look, but not by much." A small smile tugs at the corner of his mouth. His full lips are pale, I notice now. There's wisdom behind his young eyes.

"Go on, astound me." I take another bite of chicken.

"I've been this age for ten years. If you take my meaning."

I nod while I chew. This can't be real. And yet here I am, eating as I walk through Edinburgh beside the walking, talking proof I've longed for. Young and not so young.

"And what age is that?"

"Twenty-seven." A small smile tugs at the corner of his lips again. Why am I noticing that? I try to shake loose the blooming attraction.

"And did you choose to become this?" I eat slowly,

my appetite lacking. I'm far more interested in the conversation.

"I did." He looks away and presses his lips together as if he wants to say more. I wait. "But nothing really prepares you for the transformation."

"So now you'll be young and beautiful forever?"

He nods, slowly, guarded. "It was inconvenient, actually. All charm and no gravitas. People don't take me seriously."

"I do."

The words slip out before I can check them. He catches them just the same. A flicker of something crosses his face—interest? Amusement? Hunger?—and then vanishes.

"That's why you were chosen," he says softly. "You see things others dismiss. You ask the questions no one else dares to voice aloud."

"That," I say, meeting his gaze, "is because I'm not afraid of being wrong. Or right."

Silence stretches between us.

He slows his pace, our quick exit now a leisurely stroll. But there's a contained energy about him now—like a man trying not to move too quickly. Like a predator keeping his teeth hidden.

"You're curious about me," he says at last.

"You're an impossible creature offering chicken wraps," I say dryly. "Of course I'm curious."

That draws a real smile from him. It makes him look younger. Less guarded.

"Then ask."

I pause. There are so many things I want to ask. But it makes sense to get straight to the point.

"Do you drink from humans?"

His lashes lower just a little. "I do."

I don't flinch. I won't give him that satisfaction. But my pulse spikes.

"Don't your kind feed on blood bags these days?"

He gives a low hum of amusement. "We do. We have options. But nothing is as potent—or as pleasurable—as drinking from the source."

A pause.

Too long. Too loaded.

"Is it painful?" I ask.

"For whom?" His voice is velvet now. Thick with implication.

My mouth goes dry.

Darius comes to a halt and I stop beside him. He turns to face me and leans closer. Not close enough to touch, but closer than he should be. His voice drops low.

"It can be exquisite, Katrina. If done right. If invited."

The air feels warmer, tighter. I swallow, willing my heartbeat to slow.

"And if it's not invited?"

His smile fades.

"Then it's a violation. And we don't tolerate those."

I nod once, sharply. I don't know whether I'm relieved or disappointed by the answer. I should be asking him about mythological correlations or long-lost tombs. Instead, I'm wondering what it would feel like to let him bite me.

He watches me for a moment longer, then resumes walking. I fall into step beside him.

When we reach the dark door up to my flat, I turn the key then pause in the recess and turn to look at him.

"What are the rules?" I ask, keeping my voice low.

"Rules?" he replies, frowning and giving me his full attention.

"You know, sunlight, garlic, stake to the heart? I already know you don't cast a reflection. What else? Can you come in without an invitation?" Why am I asking that?

"Oh. Those rules. Well, I can't tell you about how to hurt us. Obviously." He shrugs one shoulder and almost smiles. I try not to smile back. "But I will tell you that garlic and crosses are just myths. And we do indeed require an invitation to enter a private dwelling. However," he leans close to me, pressing me back against the door. My pulse flutters and I avert my gaze. "You don't own this place. It's his. Sorry." He unlatches the door and pushes it open, causing me to stagger backwards. I quickly regain my footing and cluck my tongue in consternation.

"Sleep well, Dr Cavendish." Darius turns and stalks away into the night, slowly enough for me to watch him walk away.

I take a deep breath and step into the narrow stairwell. I lock the door and retreat up the stairs and into the flat. I'm unsettled to know that vampires can come and go at will from this place. I lock the flat door anyway. I do a sweep of the apartment, making sure the windows are locked, before heading into the kitchen and pouring myself a glass of red wine. I'm aware of the irony. I don't know if I'm holding it together or simply pretending well enough to fool myself.

The deep sofa in the living room invites me to settle on it with my wine, a soft blanket and the mysterious book with my name inside. I open it at the bookmark, sip the wine and begin reading about a psychic trapped in a haunted house. I probably shouldn't read a scary story, given what I've just been through, but I'm hoping it'll put my own dilemma into perspective.

The weight of the day presses down on me and the wine clouds my head much quicker than it normally would. The soft lighting fades around me and the sofa sucks me down into a deep sleep while a ghost's fingers brush through my hair.

I'm dreaming.

I know it even as I sink deeper, even as the warmth against my skin becomes touch, and that touch becomes him.

Not a character from my book. Not Darius.

No.

This is colder. Older. Hungrier.

Hands glide over me, too confident to be real—fingertips tracing the line of my throat, the dip of my collarbone, the curve of my waist like a map he's memorised.

I try to open my eyes, but the dream won't let me.

It wants me to feel. A whisper against my ear; a low, velvet-wrapped threat.

"You tremble for the truth, Katrina. But your body —your body already knows mine."

I try to speak but the words slip away, drowned by sensation. My skin tightens with goosebumps. A cool mouth finds my throat and lingers. Not biting. Not yet. Just breathing me in like I'm already his. His breath smells of something ancient—like parchment scorched in fire, or blood turned to ink.

My hips arch of their own accord. I'm not being touched there. Not yet. But the promise of it coils between my legs like a promise draped in silk.

"You asked how it feels," he murmurs. "Let me show you."

A tongue—warm and firm—traces the hollow of my neck, and suddenly my wrists are pinned. Not roughly. But with the kind of strength that tells me fighting would be a performance. He could break me if he wanted to.

But he doesn't. He wants me to want it. He wants me to beg.

I moan; quiet, embarrassed, half a protest. He answers with a chuckle that drips heat into my core.

The kiss that follows isn't on my lips. It's lower. Slower. A trail of kisses down my sternum, my stomach, my thighs—and then a bite. Not real. Not deep. Just teeth pressing into flesh, marking me.

Claiming.

And then—

I wake with a gasp, sweat cooling on my skin, my thighs slick, my pulse pounding like I've run miles. I'm alone on the sofa. Of course I'm alone. The faint scent of wine lingers in the air. And on the inside of my wrists, two faint impressions like the ghost of hands squeezing too tight.

I stare at my wrists.

The marks are faint. Gone, if I stare too long. But I saw them. I felt them.

I sit up slowly, the blanket sliding off my legs. My skin is flushed, hypersensitive, like I've been touched in places no one has touched in a long time. My wine sits half-finished on the table. The book still lies open, a few pages further than I remember reading.

I clutch the throw around me and rise on unsteady legs. Every creak of the floorboards makes me flinch.

*Get a grip, Cavendish.*

It was a dream. Just a dream. A perfectly logical reaction to everything I've been immersed in. The archives. The bar. The monsters—because that's what they are, no matter how charming or beautiful.

But my body doesn't feel fooled. It remembers.

I move through the apartment, double-checking the locks, even though I know it's pointless. If he wanted to come in, he could. The thought sends a fresh shiver through me.

Eventually, I force myself into the shower. I scrub my skin like it might scrub away the dream. It doesn't. The ghost of his voice flows over my skin and down the drain.

## CHAPTER FOUR

The next morning intrudes upon the sleep I so desperately need. Grey light tugging open my sleep-crusted eyes.

I wake tangled in sheets I don't remember pulling over myself, the faintest imprint of his voice still clinging to the back of my mind like a perfume I can't place. I feel... raw. Drained. Like something fed on me in the night—no marks, no proof, but the sensation lingers. My skin feels borrowed. My body, used. And yet... I'm alone.

I glance at the time and curse under my breath. I'm late. Although, given the hours that my client keeps, perhaps it doesn't matter.

The sky outside is grey and damp, Edinburgh cloaked in that endless half-light that makes the hours blur. I throw on a soft jumper and jeans, finger-comb my hair into something passable, and grab my coat. No time for breakfast, but there's a little café on the corner.

I slide inside, order the strongest coffee they have, and cradle it like medicine as I make my way towards Thirst.

The warmth seeps into my fingers. But not my chest. Not my thoughts.

Even in daylight, the street feels like it's keeping a secret.

I rap lightly on the glass door and wait. It's barely ten, and the bar is shuttered and silent. When the door finally opens, Lenora stands there like a monolith carved from disdain. She doesn't speak—just steps aside and lets me in with a nod colder than the wind outside.

"Morning," I say, offering a polite smile.

She doesn't respond. Of course not. I can't tell if Lenora wants me out of the archive or in deeper. Either way, she's not just staff. She's watching me. Reporting, maybe.

I descend to the archive alone.

It takes a while for the lights to warm up. The air down here is thick with silence, and for the first hour, I make almost no progress. My eyes skip lines. I translate words I already know, over and over. Half a sentence later, I've forgotten what came before.

My coffee is the only thing keeping me going and it's gone too soon. I don't particularly want to face Lenora's icy demeanour, so I stop myself from going upstairs to seek out a fresh cup. My hands shake when I try to take notes. I close the book and press my palms to the table, trying to ground myself. But every flicker of shadow, every breath of movement at the edge of my vision makes my skin prickle.

I can't stop thinking about the dream. The bite that wasn't. The hands that held me down. The voice that carved itself into my bones. I tell myself it was just my imagination. But then why do my thighs still ache?

I skip lunch. Forget to hydrate. By early afternoon, my head throbs behind my eyes and my limbs feel like they've been filled with wet sand.

That's when I hear the soft knock.

I look up, half-expecting no one to be there—but Darius leans in the doorway, a faint frown creasing his otherwise unreadable face.

"You look pale," he says. "Did you eat today?"

I open my mouth to lie. I fail.

"No." My admission comes with a the sudden dropping of a lead weight in the pit of my stomach.

He disappears without another word, and I slump back in my chair. I should be annoyed. But the air feels warmer where he stood. Steadier.

When he returns, it's with a tray containing a hot sandwich cut into halves, a bottle of water, and a small lemon tart tucked into the corner like an afterthought.

He sets it down gently beside me, then leans on the arm of my chair, his gaze level with mine. "Eat. Please." There's no command in his voice this time. Just quiet concern. And that's somehow worse. Because it cracks something open in me. Something softer than I want to admit.

I pick up half the sandwich. It's warm. Crisp on the outside, gooey cheese and tomato on the inside. My stomach growls in response and Darius's mouth curves ever so slightly.

"You didn't have to—" I start, but he shakes his head.

"I did. You can't fall apart in here, Katrina. He'll sense it."

I blink. "Thorne?"

He nods once, eyes dark.

"I'm not falling apart," I say, even as I eat like I've been starving for days.

"You are," he says, voice low. "And it's not your fault."

I pause mid-bite. "What does that mean?"

He straightens, but doesn't answer. Instead, he moves around the table, adjusting the lamp so it casts softer light across the pages. "The dreams will get worse," he says finally. "If you don't ground yourself."

I halt and gaze up at him. "Dreams?"

His eyes flick to mine. "I had them too. After he first set his sights on me. They're seductive. They're meant to be. That's how he gets in."

I chew slowly. Swallow. My chest tightens.

Silence stretches between us again. It hums. Like something alive, just beneath the surface. There are so many things I want to ask, but this probably isn't the best place to question Darius's loyalty to my host.

"Thank you," I say, finally. "For the food. And the honesty."

He shrugs one shoulder. "I'll always tell you the truth. Even if he doesn't."

He turns to leave, then hesitates. Glances over his shoulder.

"You should try the tart," he says, softer now. "It's the best thing on the tray."

I wait until he's gone, then pick up the tart.

And smile.

By the time the day edges toward evening, I've made progress—but not nearly enough. My notes are scattered, my brain foggy, and my limbs feel strangely heavy. The food helped. So did the warmth of Darius's voice. But the pressure is building again. A sense that I'm being watched, even underground.

So when the knock sounds on the heavy door again, my pulse leaps.

Darius steps into the doorway without waiting for an answer to his knock. He says nothing at first—just stands there, expression unreadable, until I push my chair back and look up.

"You're working too hard," he says softly.

"I don't know about that. I haven't felt very productive today."

He crosses the room, movements liquid and precise, and leans back against the table beside my notes.

"I come bearing an invitation."

I hesitate. "From Thorne?"

He nods.

"And if I don't accept?"

Darius's jaw tenses. "Then he'll wait. And keep

asking. And it will get harder to say no."

"That sounds like coercion."

"That's what he does. He doesn't command. He invites. Entices. Makes it feel like your idea."

I meet his gaze. "And you? What are you doing?"

"I do what I'm asked to do." He offers the barest smile. "And occasionally what I want."

"What am I invited to?"

"An evening of festivities. He asks that you dress accordingly."

My throat tightens.

"What exactly does 'accordingly' mean?"

"Whatever makes you feel powerful."

The air in the archive feels thinner than it did a few minutes ago.

"What exactly happens at these festivities?" I ask.

Darius's mouth lifts at one corner.

"That depends on who's watching. And what you choose to show." Darius steps back and gestures to the door. "Let me walk you home."

I gather my things and follow him up to the bar and out into the street. We walk in silence at first. The evening has turned sharp, the mist heavier. The street lights cast golden haloes on the damp pavement. Darius keeps a pace that matches mine exactly—never too fast, never too slow. Always just close enough to feel like protection, but never like possession.

After a while, I speak.

"How long did it take you to stop feeling…

unmoored?"

He tilts his head. "When Thorne turned me, you mean?"

"When you first realised what he was capable of."

"I haven't."

I glance at him.

He's watching the pavement, his hands tucked into the pockets of his coat.

"He's my sire. My master. But he's not my god. That helps."

"Do you ever regret it?"

His brow creases. "What? Becoming what I am?"

I nod.

"No." His answer is immediate. But quieter, he adds, "Not for myself."

I try not to let my thoughts linger on the meaning of that sentence. "What were you before?" I ask.

"A solicitor." He cracks a smile, a warm one, not one of a predator.

"Well, that's different." I try not to laugh.

"He needed my services. I believe my predecessor met with an accident." His voice is cool, detached. Everything he doesn't say presses against his words and I'm back on edge again.

We turn a corner. The door to my building looms ahead, shadowed and slick with rain.

"He wants something from me," I say, voice low. "And it's not just translations."

We come to a halt at the door up to my flat. Darius

fixes his cool eyes on me.

"Yes."

"What is it?"

"I don't know," he admits. "But he plays the long game, Katrina. Just be careful which pieces you offer him."

His words coil in my chest like smoke. If this were a myth, Thorne would be the underworld king. Darius, the ferryman. And me? The foolish scholar who dug too deep. I unlock the door, then turn back to him.

"Will you be there tonight?"

He hesitates. Then nods. "Somebody has to catch your glass when it falls."

I smile, but it falters quickly. "What if it's not a glass that shatters?"

"Then I'll help you gather the pieces."

That gets me. I stare at him for a beat too long. Then I nod, push open the door, and disappear into the stairwell.

## CHAPTER FIVE

The bar is busy when I arrive. Human patrons crowd the tables, laughter and clinking glasses creating a warm buzz. If not for what lies beneath, Thirst might seem like any other fashionable Edinburgh bar. But I know better.

I fit right in with this crowd. A black dress, sleek as poured ink, hugs me like a secret I'm not ready to confess. It's bold. Backless. The hem cuts mid-thigh, and the neckline plunges just far enough to make my reflection feel like a dare. My heels click a warning across the floor as I move. Assured. Unapologetic. But I'm not here for this crowd. I'm not sure if I'll fit in when I get downstairs. But fitting in doesn't seem to be a requirement.

I don't know who I'm trying to impress.

Not Thorne. He sees through everything.

Not myself. I'm not easily shaken.

Which leaves—

No.

I'm not thinking about Darius.

Even if I catch myself wondering what he'll think when he sees me like this. Even if I took an extra ten minutes on my make-up, painting my lips a bold shade of defiance.

I weave through the crowd to the corridor with the mirrored wall. I step into it and am greeted by a tall and elegant young man, dressed in a tailored suit so sharp it could draw blood. His skin is pale and his eyes are dark, inhuman.

"Dr Cavendish. You are expected," he says.

He steps in front of the mirror, and I'm not remotely surprised to see only myself reflected back. I look good. Dangerous. Like someone who might survive this.

The panel slides aside, revealing the lift, and I step inside, heels clicking on the smooth floor. I make my way, alone, into the heart of Thirst.

The lounge is dimmer than before. Softer. The furniture is pushed back, the space transformed into something ritualistic. Anticipatory.

Where before it felt like a den of secrets, tonight it is a stage. Velvet drapes have been pulled wider, revealing carved stone and flickering torches. Gold thread shimmers through deep crimson fabrics. Masks gleam on the faces of guests—half-hidden eyes, and full, painted lips. Music floats in the air like perfume—slow, seductive, with a heartbeat of something older underneath.

My entrance is noticed, like before, and heads slowly turn in my direction. For a moment, no one moves.

And then he sees me.

Darius.

He's across the room, half-turned, mid-conversation. His mask is simple—matte black, shaped like a raven's beak, sharp at the nose and elegant at the edges. It makes his eyes look brighter. Hungrier. But the second his eyes meet mine, everything else fades. His gaze sharpens. Fixes. I feel it like touch—warm and deliberate. He doesn't smile. Doesn't speak. Just watches.

Like I'm the only person in the room.

A beat passes. Then he begins to move toward me, parting the crowd without effort. Heads turn. Whispers bloom. But I only have eyes for him.

God help me—I want him to see me.

Not just look.

See.

And I think he does.

Halfway to me, he plucks something from a side table—an ornate mask of black lace and gold filigree. As he nears, he holds it out to me.

"For you," he says softly.

I reach for it, and our fingers brush. A spark lights me up inside. Nothing explosive. Just a jolt—sharp enough to draw breath, soft enough to question. Danger curls in the space between us. Not the kind that says run. The kind that says stay. Burn.

My fingers close around the mask, but I don't pull away.

"Thank you," I murmur, the words low, uncertain.

He watches me for a beat too long. His voice is velvet, edged in something darker.

"You look… dangerous."

My lips curve into a smile. "Good."

I raise the mask and tie it in place, hiding the heat in my cheeks. But I know he saw it.

He steps aside and offers me his arm.

"Shall we?"

I take it, letting him guide me into the room. The scent of wine and blood and waxy candle smoke curls around us. The music deepens. A low, pulsing rhythm that seems to sync with my pulse.

We don't speak, not at first. We simply exist in the hum between eye contact and proximity. He leads me through a narrow arch and up a curving stairwell onto a dimly lit mezzanine that overlooks the main lounge below. From this height, it's easier to take it all in—the flicker of candlelight against carved stone, the rich reds and golds of velvet drapery, the gleam of masks catching firelight.

Below us, vampires and their thralls move like silk through shadow. Some dance—slow, sensual, hypnotic. Others feed in plain sight, mouths pressed to throats, fingers clutching skin. No one pretends. Desire and danger blur until they are indistinguishable.

Up here, the hush feels intentional. A place made for watching. Judging. Anticipating.

"This is my favourite spot," he murmurs, settling beside me. "Not so many eyes. But enough."

He turns slightly to face me. His thigh brushes mine. A deliberate touch or a crowded one? I can't decide. My body is already too aware of his.

"You clean up well, Dr Cavendish," he says. "I almost didn't recognise you."

"That's the idea," I reply, voice softer than intended.

He studies me. I feel it more than see it. My breath shallows.

"Have you ever danced with danger?" he asks.

I arch a brow. "I think I'm doing it right now."

He smiles. "Then let me make it worth your while."

He leans in, so close I can smell something sharp and clean on his skin. My pulse thuds. I know this is a mistake. And I don't care.

He brushes my long hair off my shoulder, exposing my slender neck. His lips don't quite touch my skin. Just hover. The electricity between us spikes.

And then—

The spell breaks. Darius freezes. Straightens. He looks down toward the throne where Thorne is holding court. A flicker—not in his expression, but in the tension that tightens his body, like a cord pulled taut.

I glance at him, but he isn't looking at me. His gaze is distant, fixed on his sire.

Whatever just happened, I wasn't part of it.

He pulls away from me slowly and draws an

unnecessary breath. Then he murmurs, almost regretfully, "You're summoned."

I glance down towards my host, picking him easily out of the throbbing crowd. He's sitting like a shadow, all in black, his silver eyes fixed on us. One hand lifts in a beckoning gesture. His expression is unreadable.

I don't move.

Darius offers me his hand. His voice drops to a whisper meant only for me.

"I shouldn't have done that. He doesn't like to share."

My fingers tighten on his for a moment.

"Don't I have a say?"

He looks at me with an expression that might be pity, or regret. He doesn't answer my question.

Together, we return to the lower floor and cross the lounge toward the monster who owns this place. And, increasingly, owns a little more of me each day.

Thorne stands apart from his coterie now, watching our approach. The moment we're within reach, his eyes cut to Darius, gleaming like steel in candlelight.

"Darius," he says, smooth as ever, but with an edge buried deep beneath the velvet. "You may go."

It's not a request.

Darius inclines his head in a shallow bow. He doesn't look at me.

"Yes, my Lord."

I flinch at the title, but Thorne doesn't react. He steps closer to me, gaze flicking over the lace mask, the dress, the way my hair brushes my shoulders.

"You dressed for power," he murmurs. "It suits you."

"I didn't do it for you."

"No," he agrees. "That's what makes it work."

He circles me once, a leisurely prowl, and when he stops behind me, I feel him lean in. Not touching, not quite, but present. Dominant.

"You should be careful with Darius," he whispers, voice low near my ear. "He forgets sometimes where his loyalties lie."

"Does he?" I murmur. "Or do you simply not like to be challenged?"

Thorne chuckles. "Touché."

He steps around me again and offers his arm—not as Darius did, politely, supportively—but like a dare.

"Come. Let me show you what it means to dance with danger."

And like a fool—or maybe a queen—I place my hand in his.

The music shifts as we step into the space. A rhythm I feel more than hear. The crowd parts. And Thorne begins to move.

I follow. The hunter and the scholar. The monster and the girl who found him. The story begins again.

He doesn't touch me at first. He doesn't have to. His presence curls around mine like smoke, coaxing my body into movement. I fall into step as though I've done this before. As though I was made to. I've never been graceful. But tonight I feel like something else entirely.

A creature born of ink and hunger and velvet shadows.

He watches me. Not the way Darius did—warm and wanting—but like a king considering the stars. Curious. Patient. Possessive.

And I can't help it. I compare them.

Darius is comfort. A flame in the hearth. A steadying hand when the darkness bites.

But Thorne—

Thorne is the dark. He is the bite.

He leans in, lips brushing the shell of my ear. "You want to know the truth, Katrina. That's why you came."

I say nothing. I don't have to.

"You crave it. Secrets. Answers. Proof that the world is stranger than they let you believe."

My breath hitches.

"I can give it to you," he says. "All of it. Myth, memory, meaning. I will show you the bones beneath the stories. The roots of power."

I meet his eyes, my pulse thudding.

"In exchange for what?"

His lips curl. "Only your curiosity. Your honesty. And perhaps, in time, your loyalty."

He spins me, then pulls me close, hand pressed to the small of my back. My body remembers the dream. My blood sings. And the dance goes on. In a moment of dizzying boldness, I lift my chin and look into his strange, silver eyes.

"Don't you want my blood?"

He presses his body against mine, his hand on my

back holding me firmly in place. He meets my gaze as we sway and swirl through the crowd. He's not wearing a mask. His is the only face in the whole place uncovered. He is lord and master of this domain and I am his willing play-thing. At least, I think I'm willing. This isn't like me. I could be under his control already and not even know it. But something about the way my thoughts dance between him and Darius, between this place and my work, tells me that I am thinking for myself, however confusing my thoughts may be.

"I do, Katrina," he says at last. His gaze rakes down my neck before returning to my eyes. We've stopped dancing, I realise. When did that happen? The crowd moves around us but all I see his him.

"But you need more, don't you? You need more from me than that. Or you would have bitten me already."

A smile creeps across his lips, sinister and yet alluring.

"That is precisely what I want. Your sharp mind. Your wicked tongue, unafraid to cut to the truth." His fingers wrap around my neck, his thumb pressing into the soft spot just under my chin, tilting my head up. "And I want you to ask for it, Katrina. I want to hear you say the words."

The music throbs through the floor and into my body. The swirling crowd around us presses closer. His visit to me in my dream swims through my thoughts, the way he touched me... bit my thigh... I do want more. I'd be lying if I denied it and he'd see right through it. But I want Darius to kiss me, to touch me, to hold me.

The answers Thorne is tempting me with may not be enough.

As if he's reading my every thought, Thorne pulls back, releasing my neck.

"You're not ready. But I can wait, my dear."

I blink and he's gone, swept away with the mass of bodies around us. I stand alone in the middle of the dance floor and feel eyes on me from all around. Predators pressing closer. Their master no longer protecting me from their greedy mouths. Their eyes glitter like knives. Their smiles are too wide. And I realise—they smell me. Not just my fear. My desire.

A gasp rushes past my lips and I bolt for the exit, pushing through the crowd. It suddenly hits me just how many vampires are here. Dozens? A hundred? More? All in one city. Terror rushes through my veins. How little awareness humanity has of the monsters surrounding us. Panting for breath, I reach the velvet curtain and push past it into the dark corridor leading to the lift and safety.

I stumble in my high heels as I dash for the end of the corridor. I press the button repeatedly, too afraid to look back. The door glides open and I rush inside the panelled lift. I turn to press the button that will take me back to the safety of the human bar above the vampire lounge, when a dark blur sweeps past me in a gust of air.

Hands grasp me and press me to a firm chest, cradling my head and back. Thorne is gone. But the imprint he left pulses beneath my skin. And then Darius is there, wrapping me in a warmth I don't trust—but want anyway.

"I've got you, you're safe." Darius's voice is soft and soothing. The lift door swishes shut beside us and my trembling body relaxes, melting into his arms. But my mind reminds me what he is and I tense up again at once.

"Am I?" My voice is muffled against his suit. I pull back and look into his cool eyes. "You're one of them."

"I don't want to hurt you." He gazes down into my face and I search his for the truth behind his words. His mask has been discarded. His hair is slightly ruffled. Heat builds beneath my skin. His hands glide up over my arms and shoulders and he pushes the mask up off my face, his thumbs lingering on my cheeks. He leans closer, his eyes closing as his lips brush against mine.

I stiffen, unsure what on earth is happening. But just as I melted into his arms a moment ago, I surrender to the craving in my body and return the kiss. I slip my hands around the back of his neck and press my body against his.

Blood rushes through my body, warming parts of me that have been neglected of late. Our tongues press together, his hands grip my back and the back of my head.

The lift slows to a halt and the doors open beside us. We rip apart and I stumble backward, gasping for breath. The vampire in the corridor turns to face us, his narrow eyes assessing the situation. Darius takes my hand and leads me into the corridor, passing his colleague with a small nod. I cast my gaze down and scurry along in Darius's wake. He leads me through the packed bar and out into the cool street, bathed in the night.

He turns and pushes me against the wall next to the door. His eyes rake my bare skin, hunger bleeding into them. My heart races and the little part of my brain that can still form thoughts wonders how aware of my pulse he is. Can he hear it?

"Do you want this?" His voice is low and husky, thick with need.

"Yes," I whisper back. "But what will Thorne do?"

"I don't care." His mouth crashes against mine again, kissing me with hunger and desire unlike anything I've felt before. And, foolish as it might be, I brush aside all thoughts of consequences and let desire drown the voice that still whispers danger.

## CHAPTER SIX

Darius backs me into his apartment, his mouth still feverishly claiming mine. His keys clatter as he tosses them onto a table just inside the door. My heels thud warmly on the hardwood floor. I drop my clutch onto the table next to his keys without breaking our frenzied kiss. My newly freed hand threads through his hair, the other clinging to his back.

It had been a slow stumble back to his place from Thirst, stopping to kiss in doorways every few meters. Luckily, it wasn't that far from the bar. Now, here in the privacy of his home, all inhibitions are dropped.

His hands clutch at my back, my thighs, my backside. Impatient. Indulgent.

My back bumps against a wall and Darius pins me there. His hands move to cup my face and his kiss slows to a sensual exploration of my mouth.

A moan rises from my chest. I pull my mouth from his and tilt my head back, tempting him with my neck. I haven't forgotten what he is, but any sense of risk that I felt back at Thirst has evaporated and all I feel now is exhilaration. I want to know what it feels like. I want it all.

But Darius slows, he pulls back from me, his fingers trailing down over my neck and shoulders, his eyes feasting on my skin.

"You think you know what you want, but I have to be sure you're prepared." His voice drips with heat. His fingers skim up and down my bare arms.

"So prepare me," I reply, a challenge in my cocked eyebrows.

He kisses my collarbone softly, slowly. His tongue darts out and flicks across the sensitive skin. I gasp. But all too soon, the contact is broken again.

"It hurts, the bite. That's unavoidable. Wherever it happens." One finger traces the curve of my neck and down over the swell of my breast above the low neckline of my dress. His other hand runs up my inner thigh, sneaking beneath the hem of my dress.

I bite my lower lip and try not to fall apart.

"But with the pain comes pressure, then ecstasy, especially when paired with sex." His lips brush across the delicate skin of my neck as he whispers. "If the vampire gets carried away, which happens more than we like to admit, too much blood loss can have serious consequences. Including death, Katrina. One of us could kill you."

A whimper escapes my parted lips with the sensation of his light touch on my inner thigh and the ghost of his lips on my neck. I hear the words, but don't fully comprehend them. The risk feels worth it in this moment.

"You will need time to recover afterwards. You will need to hydrate, and rest. And above all, not be bitten again until you've restored your blood level. Do you understand me?"

I nod, but it's automatic. He's still touching me, still seducing me, even with the warning. He wants this as much as I do.

"You need to say it," he says, his voice and his touch firmer.

"I understand. Darius, I want you to bite me."

He steps back and tugs me away from the wall. His eyes blaze with hunger and heat. His fingers deftly go to the zip at the back of my dress and slide it slowly down to the small of my back. He trails his hands up my back on either side of my spine and slips his fingers under the spaghetti straps of my dress. Slipping them down over my shoulders, he slowly relieves me of the dress, letting it pool at my feet. He glances down at my lacy, black underwear and a low groan rushes from his throat.

I'm not the slender young thing that I was in my twenties. I have curves. I have scars. I've lived and my body bears the marks. I'm not ashamed of that, but no one has looked at me the way he is now in a very long time. Like he's been trapped in the desert for days and I'm a mirage of cool water.

Darius takes my hand and leads me into his apartment proper, away from the short hall. The studio is on the top floor of slightly crooked house and has been refurbished some time in the last decade. Although the floors are slightly curved, the furnishings are modern. Thick blinds cover every window in the open plan living space and low, amber lights peek out from below half the surfaces in the room. He leads me straight through the living room and through a door on the opposite side to the striking black and chrome kitchen. The door leads into a large bedroom, lit only by more of those hidden lights, but these are red, flooding the room with a sinister glow.

As far as I can tell, the walls are painted black. The large, low bed sits in the centre of the wall opposite the door, dominating the room. The dark wood of the floor gleams under the red lights, making it look almost like a large, red pool.

Before I can think too much about this, or change my mind, Darius pulls me flush against his firm body and presses his mouth to mine again. His hands go to my back and mine to his. My head swims with the scent of his cologne—clean, sharp, and oddly nostalgic—and the feel of his tongue probing my mouth. I hurriedly push his suit jacket off his shoulders and toss it to the floor. My fingers scramble with the buttons on his crisp, grey shirt until I find his skin. I tug the shirt down his arms and run my hands over the firm muscles of his chest. He's lean and athletic, but not built like a body builder. I rake my gaze over his upper body and draw my bottom lip between my teeth.

A grin spreads over his lips and the dimple in his left cheek deepens.

"Like what you see?"

"I do. Do you?"

He glances down my body and swiftly meets my gaze again, his smile fading to that greedy expression again.

"Absolutely. You're perfect."

Heat rises in my cheeks.

He pulls me against him again and brushes his fingers through my hair. My heart races and my breath quickens even as his movements slow. His fingers run lightly down my back, tuck into my underwear and tease the elastic slowly over the swell of my hips. He lowers himself to his knees as he slides down the lacy garment and I rest my hands on his shoulders as I step out of my shoes. He glances up at me before leaning closer and placing a soft kiss on one thigh, then the other.

In a flash, he stands and scoops me into his arms, hitching my legs up to wrap around his middle. A giggle bursts from my lips and I cling to him as he whisks me over to the bed. He throws me onto it and the laughter dies in my throat. Darius moves like a panther, lowering himself onto the bed and crawling up my body where I lay sprawled and panting. He hovers above me, his gaze roaming over my naked body before settling on my throat.

I'm desperately trying to control my breathing, but the way he's looking at me is making it impossible. I'm a meal. Fuck. This is really happening.

A clink of a belt and rustle of fabric drags my attention down between our bodies. He's unfastening his trousers. I move my hands to help, suddenly more eager and hungry myself. Together we shed him of his remaining clothes and his hard cock presses against my thigh as he lowers himself onto me, resting on his elbows. He kisses me, slowly, deeply. This is a man with all the time in the world. But I'm impatient. I wrap my legs around him and shift my hips so that the head of his cock is resting against my slick entrance.

He breaks the kiss and lifts his head slightly. "Not yet."

"I need you." The desire cracks my voice.

"Hmm, I can tell." His voice is a low rumble that vibrates through me. He rolls his hips, rubbing the tip of his shaft across where I need it.

I groan and tip my head back, exposing more of my neck. I don't regret it.

His lips caress the smooth skin of my throat. His tongue takes a long, languid stroke at it, from collar bone to jaw.

My whole body responds, writhing beneath him. My entrance is so wet now that there probably won't be any friction when he finally enters me. A shudder runs through me.

"Fuck," I whimper. "Please. I need you inside me."

A deep moan rumbles from him. "Well, seeing as you asked so nicely." He shifts his weight and pushes up onto his hands.

Our eyes meet and my breath catches as he eases into me. I hadn't appreciated how big he was from the glimpse I got. But I feel every inch now as he slides smoothly into my dripping pussy.

"Oh God," I gasp. My hands cling to his shoulders.

"I don't think he can hear you." Darius holds still, buried deep inside me, his gaze still fixed on my face.

I can't speak, I can hardly breathe. I have to force myself to take a shaking breath. I feel so full. It's been a while.

Darius begins to rock his hips, slowly pulling out of me and easing back in in a steady rhythm. I grip his sides with my knees and roll my hips in time with his. Pressure builds swiftly in my core and my breathing grows ragged. I feel everything unravelling. Decades of control and being guarded coming undone under this man, this vampire. The way his gaze bores into me as he fucks me is hot as hell. His muscles ripple with the rocking of his body, turning me on even more. As if I needed any help.

I close my eyes just to break the eye contact. I'm not used to such intensity. It's not a dream this time. I turn my head to the side as a cry rushes from my throat. My hands run down his chest and over his defined abs.

A low growl curls from between his gritted teeth and he shifts his weight onto one hand. With the other, he grabs one of my wrists and pins it above my head. The sudden roughness shocks me and my gaze locks back onto his eyes. There's a glint of red in them, probably from the red light in the room. Sure.

I lift my other hand as if to try and free my pinned one, but I know what I really want and Darius doesn't disappoint. He pins that wrist as well, locking them together under one strong hand of his own.

"Fuck," I gasp, my eyes flickering closed again.

Darius's weight shifts again onto the hand pinning my wrists. His other hand strokes up my chest and firmly clasps my throat. Not to hurt, not to suffocate, but a possessive gesture. He turns my head to the side and lowers his head to lick my neck again.

"Are you certain you want this?"

"Yes. Fuck yes."

His mouth opens, warm against my skin. Teeth brush the skin. Pressure. Then I feel the points of his canines, sharper than I'd observed. I hold my breath and close my eyes. Pain shoots through my neck as his teeth pierce the skin and slice through the flesh. I wince, not quite crying out. His hips rock slowly even as he bites into me. Every nerve in my body is on alert. It knows I'm under attack, but it feels too good to deny. My hips buck, my pussy clenches around him, my knees grip his sides harder. A whimper rushes from my open mouth.

Gulping sounds come from his throat. He's really drinking my blood. Fuck.

Our bodies writhe together, pressed firmly against one another as we fuck and he feeds all at once. Pleasure rushes through my entire body. Every muscle clenches, my toes curl and my orgasm gushes from my throat in a strangled cry. My back arches, pressing my front harder into him. The sensation goes on and on. Orgasm and a sweet dizziness merged into one.

My eyes peel open but black spots have appeared around the edges of my vision.

"Darius," I croak. "Stop."

With a lurch, he releases my wrists and yanks his

head away from my neck. Blood stains his lips and that red glint is still present in his eyes.

"Are you all right?"

I nod. His hips have stilled, but he's still deep inside me. Fuck, it feels good.

"I felt faint. But I'm fine. I'm good. Keep going."

His gaze flickers over my face, neck and upper body. With a small nod, he begins to thrust again, this time with his body propped up away from mine on his hands. I part my legs and rest my hands on his arms. Harder and faster he pumps, cool air moving over my body.

"Fuck," I moan. "Yes." His movements pull me swiftly back towards climax, rushing as if towards a cliff edge. I cry out as I plummet into oblivion. Every part of me burns. I slam my feet onto the mattress and buck my hips. The climax is better than I could have possibly imagined. The pressure deep within me and tearing through my whole body.

Darius's groan penetrates my mental fog as I begin to come down. I feel him swell inside me. His rocking slows and my eyes peel open to find him gazing down at me, sweat beading on his forehead and chest. He slows to a halt and my breathing steadies.

"You're fucking glorious," he whispers. He dips to kiss me, the coppery aftermath still on his lips and tongue. But I gladly take it. When we part, he peels off me and out of me and collapses onto the bed beside me.

I turn my head to stare at him in all his sated glory. There's a flush to his cheeks that I haven't seen before. Maybe I should feel used. Drained. Afraid. But instead, I feel... seen. Wanted. And that's far more dangerous.

"That was incredible," I say at last. A small laugh bubbles up inside me.

"It was. Thank you, Katrina. Thank you for giving yourself to me like that. It means more than you know." His hand slips onto my stomach and we lay like that, gazing at each other in the dark until the night wraps itself around me and pulls me into sleep.

# CHAPTER SEVEN

The room is candlelit, the air thick with smoke and shadow. The scent of old paper, crushed roses, and something darker coils through my lungs. I'm standing barefoot on cool stone, my black dress replaced by silk so thin it clings like mist, whispering across my skin with every breath.

I'm not alone.

He stands at the far end of the room, beside a high-backed chair carved with serpents. His silver eyes find me across the distance and I stop breathing. Thorne.

But he doesn't speak. He simply extends one hand —fingers long, pale, perfectly still.

I don't remember deciding to move. But my body answers. One step. Then another. The silk glides around my thighs. My feet are silent against the floor. My pulse, deafening.

When I reach him, he cups my face like I'm made of something fragile. His thumb traces the curve of my cheekbone.

"You dream of danger," he murmurs. "But you crave control."

I swallow. His other hand slides around my waist, splaying warm across my lower back.

"And yet..." he leans in, brushing his lips against my ear, "you came here. You always come to me."

His lips don't press, they graze—barely there, maddeningly gentle. A kiss without weight. A touch without time.

My body hums.

His fingers find the edge of the silk, sliding beneath. He doesn't need to look to know where I'm warm, where I ache.

"You gave your body to him," he says—not accusing, but observant. Knowing. "Will you give me your mind?"

The silk slips from my shoulders. I shiver. But not from cold.

"Tell me, Katrina..." His breath kisses my collarbone. "Will you let me in?"

I open my mouth to answer, but nothing comes. Only a gasp. His mouth replaces his words—on my throat, my breast, the inside of my wrist.

I'm melting. Dissolving.

And when his voice finds me again, it's not in my ear—but inside my skull.

"Say yes, and I'll give you everything. Secrets. Power. Truth. Say yes—and I'll never leave you alone again."

I wake with a gasp—heart pounding, thighs clenched, the echo of his touch stamped across my skin.

I blink into the low crimson light. The air is warm. Darius's body a steady weight beside me. I shift slightly. He's facing me, one arm curled around my waist even in sleep, his body completely still. No breath. I stare at him —at the softness in his features, the calm he wears in sleep that he rarely shows awake.

But all I can feel is Thorne.

His voice still curls through my head like smoke. His hands still linger on my skin. My body pulses with memory that isn't memory. My mouth is dry. My heart feels cracked open. What's wrong with me?

Guilt prickles sharp against my skin. Darius gave me everything last night—passion, safety, power without pressure. And I wanted it. I still want it. He made me feel alive in ways I'd forgotten I could. And yet...

Yet I dreamed of another man.

No. Not a man. A monster. One I invited into my mind.

I swallow, slowly peeling myself from Darius's hold and sitting on the edge of the bed. My body aches in all the best ways, but it doesn't stop the twisting in my gut.

How can I want them both?

Darius is warmth, steady hands, quiet devotion.

Thorne is shadow, hunger, the promise of ruin wrapped in silk.

One makes me feel safe. The other makes me feel seen.

And maybe that's what scares me most—that I want both. That some hidden part of me thrives on this danger. That I've gone too long denying the kind of desire that doesn't fit neatly into the world I built around facts and caution.

I press my palms to my eyes. I came here for knowledge. Proof. Something real to sink my teeth into that wasn't about men or sex or impossible choices. But now I'm in it. Caught between two predators, each circling closer. And worse still—part of me wants to be caught.

Behind me, Darius stirs.

"Katrina?" His voice is soft, drowsy.

I hesitate, then glance back at him. He blinks sleepily up at me, the sheets pooling low on his hips, his brow furrowing with concern.

"You all right?" he asks.

I lie. "Yeah. Just thirsty."

He smiles faintly. "That's understandable."

I rise from the bed, grabbing his shirt from the floor and slipping into it. I fasten a few of the buttons. It hangs loose and long, brushing my thighs. He watches me without comment, eyes shadowed with something I can't name. I want answers. I want control. But if I'm not careful, I'll give away far more than blood.

I pad quietly into the kitchen, the oversized shirt

brushing my thighs with each step. It smells like him—clean, sharp, something forested and masculine. I breathe it in as I open a cupboard, searching for a glass. The place is silent except for the faint hum of the fridge and the soft creak of wood as I move. I fill the glass from the tap and take a long-overdue drink.

The blinds are shut tight against the outside world, and I've lost all sense of time. I approach the nearest window and gently pull the edge of the heavy blind aside to peek out. Outside, the morning is crisp and cloudless. Pale sunlight casts long shadows across the quiet street. The ordinary world, still spinning. Unaware.

The creak of a floorboard behind me pulls my attention back into the flat and as I turn my body, the sunlight slices across the kitchen—and Darius winces along with a hiss of burning skin and a faint whiff of smoke.

"Shit," I mutter, releasing the edge of the blind immediately. It snaps back into place, swallowing the light. "I'm sorry."

"Not your fault," he says, voice low. He looks composed, but there's a faint tension around his mouth. "It wouldn't have killed me. Just cause a moment of unpleasantness."

I turn to face him. He stands between the kitchen island and the fridge in nothing but loose, cotton pyjama bottoms, hanging low on his hips. His sculpted upper body glistening faintly in the soft, amber lights from under the cabinets.

I struggle to find my words, but eventually manage.

"I thought vampires couldn't be in sunlight at all."

He lifts one shoulder. "Some of us can tolerate it. Briefly. When we're young." A shadow flickers in his expression. "But as the years go on, it gets... harder. Less predictable. Thorne—he hasn't seen the sun in decades, maybe longer. It would burn him to ash."

I study him. I take a slow sip of my water, letting the silence stretch. Darius doesn't push. He never does. That's part of the problem.

"I had another dream," I say finally.

He stills.

I don't look at him. I keep my gaze fixed on the condensation building on the glass in my hand.

"It felt... like an invitation."

His voice is quiet. Careful. "From him?"

I nod.

"And did you accept?"

I finally glance up. "I'm not sure."

He watches me for a moment. "But you wanted to."

It isn't a question.

I set the glass down and fold my arms. "I don't know what I want. That's the problem."

Darius steps forward, but stops just short of touching me. His voice stays level—gentle, not possessive.

"You don't owe me anything, Katrina. I knew what I was walking into. I just..." He trails off, gaze dipping to the floor. "I want you to be safe."

I laugh softly. Bitterly. "That might not be possible."

"No," he agrees. "But you can be aware. Thorne doesn't ask without reason. If he's calling to you—"

"He offered me things. Power. Truth. What does that mean? What don't I already know?"

Darius's eyes darken. "More than you can imagine. But his offer comes with a price. Be cautious. He's powerful. Seductive. But he's not what you think."

"And what do I think?"

"He looks like a man. But he isn't one. Not really. He can't be tamed."

The words settle heavy between us.

I don't answer. I can't.

Because the worst part is—I'm not sure I want to tame him.

"Isn't that true of you too?" I ask, tilting my chin up with what defiance I have remaining.

"Yes." The single word cuts deep. Darius opens the fridge and my body chills, bone deep. The fridge is almost empty but for the middle shelf, which is stacked with just one thing: blood bags.

A lump forms in my throat. The cold, hard reality of what Darius is stares me in the face.

"Where do they come from?" I ask, though I'm not sure I want to know the answer.

"They aren't stolen from hospitals, don't worry. We have willing donors." He closes the fridge again without taking anything out. "And the occasional enemy disposed off in an efficient manner."

"Humans who get too close to the truth?"

"Rarely. We tend to bring them under our influence, rather than disposing of them."

"Like me?"

His cool, blue eyes fix on me and he gently cants his head to the side.

"More often than not, it's a rival vampire who falls foul of the butcher's blade. Drinking another vampire's blood comes with certain side effects, some of which are undesirable, so we do it sparingly, but at times, it fills a need."

I move closer to him, drawn in by his lilting voice and tantalising skin. I run a hand up his body and press myself against his side.

"What side effects?"

"Memories. We see that vampire's memories. If it's an older, stronger vampire, we also absorb a little of their power. But it's temporary."

"I can see how that could be both intoxicating and unnerving." I press a kiss to his shoulder.

His hand snakes around my back and pins me against his firm body.

He exhales softly, the breath warming my temple. His hand splays wide across my lower back, fingers dragging slowly along my spine as if relearning the shape of me.

"You're dangerous when you do that," he murmurs.

"What, this?" I tilt my head and kiss his collarbone, my lips barely brushing skin.

"No." His voice drops. "Letting me believe you might be mine."

His words strike deep—part hunger, part ache. I rise onto my toes, pressing my body fully against him, and whisper against his throat, "Maybe I want to be."

His grip tightens—not painful, just certain. As if he's anchoring himself with me, or maybe anchoring me to him. I slide one hand down the hard lines of his stomach, feeling him stir beneath my palm. Still cool, but heating with anticipation.

The kitchen counter presses against my back as he guides me there, lifting me effortlessly to sit on its edge. My legs part for him, thighs bare against the chilled marble. He steps between them, hands skating beneath his shirt I'm still wearing, palms warm where they settle at my waist.

He kisses me.

God, he kisses me.

Not like last night. Not hungry. Not greedy. This kiss is reverent. Like he's memorising me. Mourning me. Worshipping me.

His hands travel higher, brushing the underside of my breasts. I arch into his touch, breath hitching when his thumbs sweep over my nipples.

"I should be stronger than this," he murmurs into my mouth. "But when I touch you, I forget how to be anything but yours."

My fingers thread through his hair and tug gently, forcing his eyes to meet mine. "Then don't be strong," I say. "Be here. Be mine."

The growl that rolls through him is soft, guttural, filled with restrained need. He sinks to his knees in front of me, hands sliding down my thighs. He pushes the shirt up around my hips and kisses the inside of my knee, then higher. Higher.

I brace myself on the edge of the counter, legs trembling, heart pounding as his mouth finds me.

His tongue is cool at first. Then hot. Then everything.

I moan—low, involuntary—as he devours me like I'm sacred and sinful all at once. Every flick of his tongue, every slow press of his mouth is a vow I don't know how to name. My hands tangle in his hair. My hips roll into his face. I feel him hum against me, pleasure blooming sharp and fast in my belly.

"Darius—" I gasp.

His hands hold me firm, his mouth relentless. He doesn't rush. Doesn't falter. He takes me apart with patience and precision. And when I shatter—when I cry out and tremble and fall—he holds me through it, still kissing me like prayer.

When I finally slump back against the cabinets, breathless and ruined, he rises slowly. His mouth glistens. His eyes burn.

"Still thirsty?" he asks, voice husky.

I reach for him with shaking fingers, pulling him into a kiss that tastes like me. "Always."

With one motion, Darius lifts me into his arms, and I let out a breathless laugh, already reaching for his mouth again. But before he can carry me even a step away from the counter, a sharp, insistent buzz breaks the moment.

His phone.

He freezes. A low growl hums in his throat.

"Don't answer it," I whisper, nipping his jaw.

But he's already lowering me gently back onto the counter, his touch lingering, reluctant. He crosses the kitchen and snatches the phone from the side table.

His jaw tightens as he reads the screen. "It's Thorne."

My breath stills. The name crashes over me like a wave of cold water.

Darius answers. "Yes." A pause. "Of course." Another pause. His tone remains steady, respectful. But I can see the subtle tension in his shoulders.

He ends the call and sets the phone down with a muted thud.

"I have to go," he says, turning back to me. "He needs me."

Of course he does.

I hop off the counter, tugging the hem of his shirt down around my thighs. I follow him to the bedroom and watch him as he fetches clothes from his wardrobe. "I'm a little surprised that he deigns to use modern technology. Can't he summon you psychically?"

Darius tilts his head slightly, studying me. "True. He doesn't need to be in the room to make himself felt. But he can only communicate with my mind fluently when we're in the same physical place. He has to call to make specific requests like this."

The dream floods back—his voice in my head, his mouth on my skin, the way he spoke like he already owned a part of me. I knew it wasn't just a dream, but now I wonder if his mental hold on me is stronger than the hold he has on Darius.

Darius is pulling on his shirt, buttoning it with crisp efficiency. But he glances at me, eyes shadowed.

"Are you all right?"

I nod, but the gesture is slow. Measured. "I think so."

He presses a kiss to my forehead. "Don't worry. We haven't done anything wrong."

"I know. I'm okay. I'll head back to my flat to change and then head to the archive. I have a lot to do."

"I would offer to escort you, but I have to—"

"I know, it's okay. Go to him. I can see myself out."

He leans in and kisses me again, slow, sensual, full of promise. And then he's gone, slipping through the door like smoke, leaving me alone in the silence that follows.

I pad to the nearest window and lift the edge of the blind again. The sky is brighter now, the world outside calm and untouched. But I don't feel calm.

I feel watched.

I feel wanted.

And as the memory of Thorne's voice coils through me once more, one thought refuses to leave:

What if he's already inside me?

# CHAPTER EIGHT

The archive is quiet, as always. The scent of dry paper and dust settles over everything, familiar and grounding. But today, it does nothing to calm me.

I spend the daylight hours going through records, sorting catalogues, and making notes I'll barely remember. My mind isn't on the job. It drifts—again and again—to last night. To Darius's mouth on mine, his voice, his hands. The reverence in his touch. The pleasure he gave me.

And then, inevitably, to the dream.

Thorne's voice curls through my thoughts like a lingering perfume. The silk against my skin. The weight of his gaze. The words he didn't whisper but still pressed into my mind. *Will you let me in?*

The hours crawl. I try to distract myself—tea, emails, meaningless tasks—but nothing holds my attention. As the clock on the wall inches closer to twilight, I find myself staring at its slow-moving hands, pulse ticking faster with every passing minute.

Something is coming. I feel it.

When I finally leave the archive and the warmth of Thirst, it's full dark. The city glimmers around me—lights glowing in windows, the hum of nightlife rising.

Darius is waiting outside.

"He's waiting for you," Darius says, his voice low. He offers me his arm. I hesitate, but his expression makes it clear I don't really have a choice. I take his arm.

We walk in silence. The route is unfamiliar—narrow alleys, hidden turns, a path carved by memory rather than maps. When we stop, we're standing before a heavy door nestled in the side of a crumbling building that looks long abandoned.

He doesn't come inside.

His eyes flicker—not quite warning, not quite regret. Something else. Something that might be longing.

"He knows everything. It's pointless trying to keep secrets. He's not going to harm you, Katrina. He wants you."

"What about you? Us?" My pulse is racing. I have no idea what any of this means. Only that my body is yearning for more.

"He's my master. If he wants you, he gets you."

"Doesn't what you want matter at all?"

"No."

"And me?"

"He'll give you a choice, but it isn't one really. Could you leave here now, knowing what you know? Do you really think he'd allow it?"

I don't answer. I know the truth, and he doesn't need me to reply. He places a soft kiss on my cheek, and it almost feels like goodbye.

I'm shaking as I push the door open.

The room beyond is dimly lit by candles set in wrought-iron sconces. Velvet drapes line the walls, muffling sound and casting rich shadows. The floor is polished wood, gleaming beneath a scattering of plush rugs. Along the walls, beneath the drapes, linger the unmistakable shapes of equipment—restraints bolted to sturdy beams, a padded bench, cuffs, collars, coils of rope. A St. Andrew's cross gleams in one corner, half-hidden by a curtain. The air is warm with the scent of incense and something more primal—something like blood and spice and smoke.

Thorne stands by a chaise longue draped in crimson fabric. He's dressed in black—always black—and his silver eyes catch the candlelight as if lit from within.

"Katrina," he says. My name on his lips is a caress.

I step inside. The door closes behind me with a soft click.

"You came."

I don't answer. I can't. My voice is caught in my throat, my body already reacting to his presence. My pulse pounds. My skin prickles.

He steps forward, slow and smooth. No threat. No rush.

"I promised you truth."

I nod. He lifts a hand and cups my cheek. His touch is cool, but it sears through me like fire.

"But truth requires surrender." His other hand slides to the back of my neck, fingers threading through my hair. I glance around at the equipment on display. Surrender, indeed.

"Look at me."

I do. His eyes hold mine, unblinking. And I feel it—the pull, soft at first, then insistent. His voice echoes not just in my ears but in my mind.

*Let me in.*

My breath hitches. I try to resist. I do. But it's like trying to fight the tide.

*You want to understand. You want to know what's real. You've always wanted more.*

My eyes flutter. His hands are the only thing anchoring me.

*Say yes.*

My lips part. The word catches in my mouth.

He leans closer, lips brushing my ear. "Say it."

"Yes."

The world falls away.

His mouth claims mine with sudden, shocking intensity. There's no gentleness here—just hunger, heat, possession. I'm not kissed—I'm consumed.

And I want it.

My hands find his shoulders, his chest. He's hard and cold and perfect. He presses me against the velvet-draped wall, his body pinning mine. I wasn't even aware of moving across the room. One hand roams down my side, slow and deliberate.

His mouth tears from mine and finds my throat. He doesn't bite. Just drags his lips over the skin he knows I'll offer. The skin I've already given to another. His lips brush over the marks left by Darius. But this is different. Deeper.

"Mine," he whispers, and it's not a question.

I don't argue.

My clothes fall from my body without effort, pooling at my feet. His hands roam freely now, claiming every inch of exposed skin.

My mind is only half present. A thick fog swirls through it, blocking out anything beyond the room and half of what's happening inside it. All I'm aware of are the sensations in my body. The way my skin tingles at his touch, the way my heart pounds, and the heat building deep inside me.

Thorne guides me and I let him. I'm dimly aware of my wrists being shackled against cool wood. Then my ankles. I'm on the cross in the corner. My skin blazes and my eyes try to focus on him, but that fog is obscuring everything.

"I won't take much, my dear. I know you've been fed on already."

His words are thick, heavy, slow. It's as if I'm hearing them from under water.

His long, slender fingers trace my breasts and run down over my stomach. He's on his knees in front of me, like Darius was this morning. But this time I'm restrained and not thinking straight. Thorne's lips caress the soft skin of my inner thigh. His fingers slide inside me and a gasp rushes from my lips.

I'm rooted back in my body and rushing rapidly towards a climax. He knows just how to touch me. Like he's known me like this before. Like he can read my every whimper and tremor.

When he finally bites my inner thigh, it's not with warning. It's not with restraint.

It's with intent.

Pain blooms. Followed by ecstasy.

And in that moment, I understand exactly what he meant by surrender.

Because I do.

Fully.

Willingly.

Utterly.

When I come back to myself, I'm no longer bound. I'm on the chaise, swathed in velvet and Thorne's robe. My limbs feel like silk—weightless, fluid. Every part of me hums. The bite on my thigh throbs faintly, but it's eclipsed by the rush flooding my system. He sits beside me, watching.

In his hands is a small, black lacquered tray. Upon it rests a tiny ceramic bowl and a delicate silver spoon.

When he dips it, golden liquid clings to the bowl—thick, amber, rich.

"Honey," he murmurs, as though the word itself is a promise. "Old magic. Restorative. A gift from the divine to the living."

I part my lips without thinking, and he brings the spoon to them, coaxing the honey into my mouth. It's warm, fragrant, impossibly sweet.

"Good girl," he purrs, stroking a lock of hair back from my face. "We must replenish what's taken."

Another spoonful. And another. The honey coats my throat, my belly, my bones. I sigh, sinking deeper into the velvet.

"You endured so beautifully," he says. "I take no more than what you offer. And you... offered so much."

I'm still under his spell. I know it. I feel it lingering in my mind, like perfume on skin.

"You meddled," I whisper, tapping my temple.

His smile is indulgent. "Of course I did. And you liked it."

I can't argue. Not really.

"I want to see you," he says, his voice softer now. "All of you. In your glory. In your strength. You don't even know what you are yet, do you?"

My brows pinch. "What I am?"

He leans close, brushing the side of my face with the back of his fingers. "You are becoming. That's what I find most delicious."

Before I can speak, the door creaks open. Darius enters.

He stops dead.

His gaze moves over me—draped in Thorne's robe, cheeks flushed, lips sticky with honey. He says nothing. But the tension in his shoulders is a palpable thing.

Thorne doesn't look at him. His gaze is fixed on me. He simply says, "You're late."

"I came as soon as I was summoned."

I glance from one man to the other, my mind still sleepy and slow, but I can feel the frisson of electricity in the air.

"Mm." Thorne finally turns, then gestures to me without taking his eyes off Darius. "Make sure she gets home safely."

I sit up, shakily. My mouth opens, but I don't know what I want to say.

Darius steps forward, quiet and composed. He scoops me up into his strong arms and I tuck my head in against his shoulder, drinking in his warm scent. I feel Thorne's eyes on me. I don't look back. But I feel him smile.

Not with kindness.

With possession.

The car ride is silent at first. Darius drives with both hands on the wheel, his eyes fixed on the road. I rest my head against the window, the cool glass soothing my overheated skin.

When he pulls up outside my building, he gets out and opens the passenger door without a word. I let him help me out and lean against him as we climb the stairs to my flat. Still unsteady on my feet.

Inside, the flat is dim and still. Darius closes the door behind us and turns on a lamp, casting a warm pool of light across the room. He guides me to the sofa, where I sink down gratefully.

He crouches in front of me, his eyes scanning my face.

"Are you in pain?"

"No," I say softly. "Just... worn thin." He's so close. I could part my knees and pull him towards me. Part of me wants nothing more, even though I'm exhausted. I still crave his gentle touch.

He nods and rises to his feet, as if sensing my thoughts and immediately throwing cold water on them.

"I'll make tea." He strides away.

I watch him move through my kitchen, fetching mugs and boiling water like he knows the space intimately. Like we've always lived in this strange rhythm.

When he returns, he hands me a mug and sits at the opposite end of the sofa. A careful distance.

"Thank you," I say. The sting of his coolness hurts more than I care to admit. Just this morning, he was tongue-deep inside me in his kitchen.

He nods, looking down at the tea he doesn't drink.

"You looked radiant," he says eventually. "When I arrived to collect you."

"Thank you." Heat rises in my cheeks. "It doesn't feel real."

"That's how he works. Makes you feel chosen."

I study his face. There's no malice. Just truth. Sadness.

"I don't know what to do," I admit.

"You can't choose anything now. You belong to him. Just rest. Recover. Be ready next time he wants you."

"What about us?"

"There is no us now, Katrina. I'm sorry."

I stare at him as tears begin to form. I hold them back. I won't spill them in front of him.

He sets down his mug, his tea untouched, and stands. "I'll leave you to sleep. Call me if you need anything."

"Will you really come if I call?"

"Always."

He presses a soft kiss to my forehead, then disappears into the night.

And I sit in the silence, holding my tea, wondering what the hell I've gotten myself into.

## CHAPTER NINE

I don't return to the archive the day after Thorne's bite. I need time to rest, to think. My body is sluggish, my head woolly, but by midday I feel something lift. Like the last of his venom has worked its way through me, leaving behind clarity in its wake. My situation is unexpected and complex, but not unwanted. I was adrift in my life. Untethered. Now I have this purpose and a challenge unlike any I've faced before. I'm here to protect secrets. To be part of something much bigger than myself. My entire worldview has shifted, opened. There is more to this world than most people will ever know. And I'm a part of that now.

I brew strong coffee, open all the blinds, and let the light spill in. The flat fills with golden warmth. I perch on the windowsill, hugging my mug, and let the sun kiss my skin. I hadn't realised how little of it I've seen since arriving in Edinburgh. So much of my time has been spent underground—either in the archive or Thirst.

I feel... strange. Not weak, exactly. But not quite myself either. As though something inside me has shifted. Been claimed.

On a whim, I pick up the book. The one that appeared in my flat, full of strange stories that feel too tailored to be coincidence. I flip through its pages, letting them fall open at random. My eyes catch on a name—Ivy. Coincidentally, the name of one of my favourite authors.

I begin to read Ivy's story. She's in love with two men.

It's not my story. Not exactly. But the resonance is there. This woman is caught between two forces, each offering her something different. One is wild, the other grounded. One wants to possess her, the other protect. Ivy doesn't want to choose. Can't choose. The story ends on a note of possibility, a decision not to choose between them. A life together despite the risks.

I set the book down slowly.

The afternoon drifts by in a haze of thoughts I can't quite pin down. I eat something small—my appetite is lacking but I know I should eat. I shower and try not to imagine hands on my skin that aren't mine. Try not to remember the taste of Thorne's kiss, or the look in Darius's eyes as he let me go.

Late in the afternoon, my phone buzzes.

A message from Darius.

*You're expected at Thirst tonight. 9pm. Dress appropriately.*

There's no sign-off. No softness. Just that cool,

detached formality. It's clearly on Thorne's behalf, not his own.

Still, my heart races.

I follow the instructions and dress to impress. I treat my lips to a rare taste of red lipstick. When I check my reflection, I hardly recognise myself. I'm not sure if that's a good or bad thing.

The club pulses with low, thrumming bass as I descend into Thirst, but tonight the music seems distant—like I'm floating above it. There's a buzz in the air that prickles against my skin, like the whole place is waiting.

And maybe it is. Waiting for me.

I step inside, and heads turn.

My heels click across the floor, echoing in the spaces between beats. My dress is a second skin—inky black, slit to the thigh, dipping low in the back. My hair cascades in glossy waves down my spine, more luminous than usual. My skin glows with a pearlescent sheen, paler than before but somehow radiant. Even I notice it. The bite of Thorne's claim, the echo of Darius's touch—it's written in my very bones.

I am changed.

I catch sight of Darius near the far wall, cloaked in shadow, watching. Our eyes meet across the space and my breath catches. There's longing in his gaze. Hunger. Pain. But he doesn't move. Doesn't speak. Just watches as I pass.

And I do pass—gliding past the bar, past the booths, past the stunned mortals and wary vampires—until I reach the alcove where Thorne sits on his throne.

Two guards step aside as I approach.

It's quieter here. More rarefied. The music is muted, the lighting dimmer. Gold and crimson glimmer in the décor like spilled treasure. And at the centre, commanding the room, sits Thorne.

He rises as I approach, lips curling into a slow smile.

"Katrina," he purrs. "My darling."

He offers his hand. I take it. He guides me to sit beside him, claiming the space at his right hand as though it were always mine. The seat is warm. Plush. I sink into it like I belong there. A drink appears in my hand before I can ask. Cool. Hydrating. Citrus and something herbal. I sip without thinking, and it soothes the lingering ache in my throat. I glance around the room. Eyes are on me. Curious. Appraising. Envious.

And then I spot her.

Lenora.

She's at the bar, dressed in black, her auburn hair pinned into an elegant twist. Her eyes are fixed on me—and they burn. She doesn't smile. She doesn't look away. She seethes.

The music shifts, dark and sensual, and Thorne leans close, his hand resting on my thigh, possessive and unmistakable.

I keep my spine straight. I sip my drink. And I meet Lenora's stare with a steady gaze of my own.

Let her burn.

Because tonight, I am untouchable.

And everyone knows it.

Thorne takes my hand and turns it over in both of his, his long, slender fingers cool to the touch. He draws my exposed wrist up to his lips and draws a deep breath, his eyelids flickering sensuously as he drinks in my scent. His lips lightly kiss the thin skin over my veins.

"Delectable, my dear. How I long to taste you again."

I should be repulsed by the intrusion. The possessiveness. But instead, a traitorous thrill coils low in my belly. I should want to run. But God help me—I want to stay. My heart thumps so hard I'm sure he can hear it. But he releases my wrist without another word and turns his attention back to the room.

I sit beside him while his court come before him one by one to curry favour, report on incidents, pay tribute, and, I suspect, get a closer look at me. I sit quietly, my legs crossed at the knee and my eyes cast down slightly. When I finish the fruity drink, another just like it appears in front of me without me requesting it. I look up to see Lenora stooped before me, her hand moving away from the glass she just placed on the table. Her ice-grey eyes are fixed on me and they pierce the armour I've crafted around myself.

I can't help wondering what her problem is as she backs away, turns and storms over to her place behind the bar. It clicks then. She's a servant. A willing one, no doubt, but her role is below mine. I'm new here and I just waltzed straight to Thorne's right hand side in a matter of days. Who knows how long she's faithfully served him. She must be jealous.

Discomfort squirms deep in my belly. I never intended to ruffle feathers in coming here. I had no idea of the viper nest I was stepping into. I came here as an academic, to learn. There was no intention to become a vampire lord's mistress, or whatever the fuck I am now.

As I sit here, on display for all to see, I suddenly feel acutely alone. No one speaks to me. They barely dare to glance at me when they get closer, but those keeping further back stare at me unabashedly, assessing me, no doubt. Whispers seem to carry my name on them, behind hands concealing mouths. I may be imagining it, but I suspect not. That disquiet moves slowly up my spine the longer I sit there.

I search the crowd for Darius, the one friendly face in the place, but he is conspicuously absent. Even Thorne notices, late into the evening.

"Where is Darius?" he demands of those stooping close to him. "I haven't seen him in hours." He rises to his feet and I watch as he slowly scans the lounge with his penetrating gaze.

"I'm here," Darius replies, loud enough that he might be standing right beside me, but when I whip my head around, there is no one there.

Thorne reacts to his voice, however, with a smile that crawls slowly over his white teeth. His canines elongate slowly as I stare at his mouth, his fangs descending from the gum to reveal themselves. I haven't actually seen that before, despite having been bitten twice now. It's equal parts fascinating and horrifying.

The crowd parts as Darius approaches and dips into a bow in front of his sire.

"What is your will, my Lord?"

I smile and try to catch his eye, but his gaze remains fixed on Thorne's feet. A stab of rejection catches me again and I swallow the hard lump forming in my throat.

"My beautiful thrall requires company."

It takes a moment before I realise he means me. How the fuck did he know that? Is he still reading my thoughts?

*Always.*

Thorne's voice inside my head cuts like a blade.

*Relax*, comes another voice. Darius. Damn. *Don't react. Just breathe.*

I look to him, but his head is still bowed.

"You will join us and keep her company while I conduct my business."

"Yes, my Lord." Darius stands and sweeps past me, taking a seat beside me. I turn slightly to face him, but he still refuses to look at me and his expression is stony. It's so different from the warmth he showed me previously that it stings all the more.

Thorne returns to his minions, apparently satisfied that he has met my need.

I clear my throat, unsure what to do. This isn't better. Especially with the knowledge that Thorne can read my thoughts as clearly as hearing my spoken words.

"So, no privacy even in my own head now, huh?" I ask Darius, not looking at him.

"Only when you're this close to him." Darius leans a little closer to be heard over the music throbbing through the stone walls. My breath quickens at his proximity and I instantly regret it, knowing it'll be observed.

"And you?" I ask. There's no point trying to conceal it. "You can read my thoughts too?"

"I can."

"Since you fed on me?"

"Yes." Still he refuses to meet my gaze. I reach for my drink and remember how he caught my glass upstairs that first day. His hand darts out and gently touches my hand before it reaches my glass. He takes it and squeezes firmly, telling me without words or thoughts, that he is still here. He remembers too.

"What does it mean?" I ask softly, afraid of my thoughts and my precarious situation.

"You're bound to us both. He knows it too. He always knows."

*He can't hear me when I project my thoughts into your mind like this. But he'll hear if you reply to me. Just keep breathing, Katrina. Keep breathing. No matter what.*

I do as he says. I take my drink and sip it slowly as I try not to let my thoughts drift.

*I want to protect you from him, but I can't. I'm as trapped as you.*

His telepathic words cut deep and my own mind

will give us away if I let it. But I understand his detachment. He's protecting me. Well, both of us, I suppose. He has skin in this game too.

"Do you and he share a bond like this?" I ask as I place my drink back on the table.

"Not quite. But similar."

"He doesn't feed on you, does he?"

"No. Not since he made me what I am."

It feels strange to be talking like this right beside Thorne, knowing he can hear our entire conversation. But when a creature can hear your very thoughts, there are no secrets. I glance towards him and find him immersed in conversation with a large, bald vampire in a suit that pulls so tight at the seams that he looks likely to burst right out of it at any moment. I catch a glimpse of Lenora moving through the room, collecting empty glasses.

"And Lenora? What is she to him?"

"His trusted aide. She runs this place and makes him money, protects his secrets."

"You know what I mean," I say, turning to face Darius. He finally meets my gaze and his eyes burn with regret. "Does he feed on her? Does he read her thoughts?"

"Does he sleep with her?"

"Well, I wasn't going to ask that, but sure." A smile tugs at the corner of my lips.

"He trusts her. He'd only put that much trust in someone he could read. So, yes, she is his thrall. Like you."

"She's jealous." I take another drink.

Darius nods. "Probably, yes. You're a threat to her."

"Do I need to be careful?"

"No. She's fine. She'll settle down when she gets used to you."

"How long has she served him?"

"I'm not sure. Longer than I've been around."

I cluck my tongue. I know very well that she won't 'settle down'. I take another drink and set the glass down.

"Twenty years," Thorne says, leaning close to my ear and making me jump. I stifle a nervous laugh. "Lenora has served me faithfully for twenty years. I trust her with my life and will brook no criticism of her." He kisses my cheek but the threat is evident. "Come, my dear. It is time we retire." He holds out a hand. I take it and get to my feet, straight into his arms. He slips them around me and kisses my neck with agonisingly slow precision. My pulse quickens at his touch. His quiet possessiveness is intoxicating.

Darius's sizzling jealousy pierces my mind but I refuse to react.

"Darius," Thorne says, moving me to his side and draping his arm around my shoulders. Darius looks up expectantly from his seat. "I trust you can wrap things up here tonight. I'll need you at first light to escort Katrina home."

"Of course," Darius replies with a small nod. His eyes narrow ever so slightly and I just know he's fighting his own mind.

"Goodnight," Thorne says before turning me and guiding me away through the crowd.

A knot of nerves turn in my gut. I don't know what he has in store for me, given that by his own admission, he can't feed on me again yet. I suspect that what I experienced last night is just touching the surface of his various needs. As much as he scares me, as much as I'm attracted to Darius, Thorne captivates me in a different way. He is cool, he acts like he owns me. But that's because he does. And somehow, despite a lifetime of liberal values, a treacherous part of me wants to give myself to him, to lose myself in him. To give him everything. Even if the price is my life.

## CHAPTER TEN

I can't check the time, but it must be long past midnight. Thorne leads me away from the lounge down a corridor that is long and silent. Ornate candle holders line the walls, each tall, black candle casting golden light over oil paintings too shadowy to make out. Thorne says nothing as we walk, his hand firm at the small of my back. His pace is unhurried, purposeful. I don't speak either. The air between us crackles with anticipation—not fear, exactly, but the sharp-edged awareness of what's to come.

He stops at a black-lacquered door and presses his palm to a panel beside it. Something clicks. The door swings open, revealing a narrow, stone stairwell leading up and lit by flickering candlelight.

"Up," he says simply.

I go ahead of him and the door thuds shut behind us. Stone walls close in around us, but the scent of beeswax and leather grows stronger. When we reach the top, I step into the room I was brought to last night. I realise, perhaps belatedly, that there must be many tunnels like that below the city that the vampires use to move around in daylight.

Thorne moves around me and leads me straight through the room and though another, wooden door.

I step through it behind him into a vast, windowless chamber with vaulted ceilings. Rich velvet drapes cover the walls in deep wine and matt black. At the centre stands a four-poster bed carved from black wood, draped in chains instead of curtains. Surrounding it, a curated array of implements: floggers, paddles, cuffs, ropes, clamps. Everything gleams. Everything is intentional.

And then I see the throne—a dark, imposing seat carved from the same black wood, inlaid with blood-red cushioning—positioned against the wall facing the foot of the bed. Thorne takes his place in it like a king surveying his domain.

"Strip," he says.

Heat flares across my cheeks, but I obey. Slowly. Sensually. I want him to see that I do this not just out of compulsion, but desire. As I bare myself to him, inch by inch, my pulse climbs steadily higher.

"You belong to me," he says, his voice low, dangerous. "But you haven't acted like it."

My breath catches.

"You question my choices. You doubt Lenora. And worst of all—" he stands and crosses the space between us in three fluid strides, cupping my chin and tilting my face up to his—"You still hunger for Darius."

I open my mouth to speak, but he shakes his head.

"No lies. Not here."

His thumb brushes over my lower lip. "I don't mind your desire for him. But you will learn where your loyalty lies. Who owns your pleasure. Who decides what you feel, and when."

My body trembles, but it's not fear. It's the crashing wave of need, curling tighter with every word.

He guides me to a leather-coated bench and bends me over it. My hands find metal handles just below where my chest presses against the padding. My buttocks are bared, vulnerable. Expectant.

Thorne shifts one of my ankles with firm hands and straps it into a leather cuff, then the other ankle. I'm rooted in place and my knees shake slightly in anticipation.

The first strike of his palm lands with shocking precision—not cruel, but firm. A sharp sting that flowers into warmth.

"Count," he says.

"One," I gasp.

The second is slower. Measured.

"Two."

Then another.

"Three." I hiss the word between clenched teeth.

"Relax your jaw," he instructs. I try to do as he says and flex my jaw muscles, allowing my mouth to hang open.

The fourth strike pierces the silence and I cry out.

"Four." My voice is little more than a whimper.

The next slap yanks my head up, my hair caressing my back, even as I moan out a pained "Five."

He pauses only to whisper against my ear.

"You're doing beautifully."

By seven, my knees wobble. By ten, I'm panting, soaked with arousal and surrender alike. His fingers stroke the heated flesh, tender and worshipful.

"Tell me who you belong to."

"You," I breathe. "Thorne. I belong to you."

There's a pause.

"That's my good girl."

He stoops to unbuckle the straps restraining my ankles. I whimper and my legs give way, collapsing my weight down onto the bench fully. My mind swims with heavy fog. Doubt and fear have no place here now.

Thorne gently lifts me as if I weigh nothing and carries me to the bed. He lays me on my back and smiles warmly, his fangs protruding ever so slightly. Then he binds my wrists over my head in soft leather cuffs and slides a blindfold over my eyes. The world narrows to sound, scent, sensation.

A brush of fur. A cool metal chain. The kiss of silk against my throat. Then cool lips against mine, claiming. Possessing. And beneath it all, a moan that I don't realise is mine until it breaks free.

He takes his time exploring every inch of my body with his slender fingers and icy lips.

And I let him.

He captures one nipple between his teeth and I hold my breath, waiting for pain. But none comes, just the flick of his tongue over the sensitive flesh. A shudder rushes through my body.

Thorne moves away from me and the cool air of the chamber brushes my skin, his absence felt by every nerve in my body. The rustle of fabric tells me he's undressing. I lie there, trying not to squirm. I'm fired up and ready to come undone and I'm left with no contact.

*Soon, my dear.* His voice is like silk in my head. It soothes me. Stills me.

His weight presses onto the bed at my feet and me moves up my body, pressing firm kisses on my thighs, my sex, my stomach. He lays on top of me, his body heavier than I expected from his slim frame. He's hard, like marble, and cool to the touch. His knees spread my thighs and he settles between them.

I'm soaked from my spanking and so ready for this. He slides his long, hard cock inside me in one fluid stroke and braces his weight on his hands on either side of my shoulders.

"Katrina," he whispers my name with reverence. "My beautiful one. You are mine, body and soul. Who does your pain belong to?"

"You," I reply, my voice catching. He's holding still inside me but the weight of him, the fullness of him inside me, is making it hard to breathe.

"That's right. And who does your pleasure belong to?"

"Also you," I say, barely above a whisper.

"Yes. Me." He begins to move, slowly rocking his hips. I draw my knees up on either side of his body and a groan escapes my parted lips. His movements are firm but supple, a rolling motion from shoulder to knee that draws him out of me and back in with exquisite precision. "Come for me, Katrina. Come undone."

I'm rushing towards climax, closer and closer with every roll of his hips.

"Fuck," I gasp, arching my back.

*I have waited centuries for you, Katrina. Now I have you. I'm never letting you go.*

His words press into my thoughts and that's it. I lose all restraint. To be desired, demanded, like this, is unlike anything I've felt before. My orgasm crashes upon me from deep inside and fills my body. My legs tense, my toes curl, and the cry that bursts from my mouth sounds totally unlike me. It's not a sound I've ever made before. But Thorne is deeper inside me than any man before him, in more ways than one, and I feel the pleasure in my bones and inside my very soul.

He keeps me coming like that until my voice is hoarse. When he finally releases me, guiding me down from the high, he cradles me in his arms, his cock still inside me. The mood shifts from feral to reverent, and in his arms, I feel something I never expected: safe.

Not owned.

Held.

I must have slept because I'm aware of waking up. My wrists are no longer bound, but the blindfold remains over my eyes and I slip it off with a shaking hand. My body is raw, used. I sit up slowly and look around the dark chamber, lit only by a few flickering candles burning low. Thorne reclines in his throne, wearing a black, silk robe, and his gaze fixed on me.

"I trust you feel well." His voice coils like smoke across the room.

"I'm fine," I reply, although it's not entirely true.

"Hmm, I thought I made it clear that I expect honesty in here, Katrina."

"I'm sorry," I dip my head and draw my knees against my chest. "I ache, I'm hungry. But I'm sure I'll be fine soon."

"Better." His cheek twitches slightly and his gaze flicks towards the door. "You should dress. Darius has just arrived to take you home."

So, it is morning. I nod mutely, shimmy to the edge of the bed and seek out my underwear and dress. They have been placed over the spanking bench. I get to my feet and hurriedly gather my things as Thorne gets to his feet and slips out through the door.

Low voices echo dully through the thick, wooden door between us and my pulse races. I don't know how to face Darius after last night. I don't know what to do with all of these feelings and the strangeness of my situation. I dress quickly and clumsily, eager to leave but also a bundle of nerves.

Once I'm somewhat presentable—although it's guesswork, as there's no mirror—I tug open the door and squeeze through the gap into the other chamber. Darius glances my way, but doesn't linger. Thorne holds a hand towards me and I move over to him, taking his hand in mine.

"Darius will see to your needs this morning, my dear. But remember the lesson from last night."

I keep my gaze on the floor, my cheeks burn. I can feel both men staring at me and my spine tingles.

"I shall see you at Thirst this evening. Both of you."

And just like that, we're dismissed. Thorne turns away, dropping my hand. Darius places an arm around my shoulders and guides me out through the door into a cool, crisp early morning light. He draws a hood over his head as he walks me to the car at the kerb. Without a word, he guides me into the passenger seat and swiftly moves around the car to slide into the driver's seat. Finally, he looks at me but I can only spare him fleeting glances. What is this feeling? Shame?

"What lesson, Kat? What did he do?"

I shake my head. I can't say. Not because of some rule, or fear. It's loyalty. Strangely.

"That's between us. But I'm fine, Darius. Absolutely fine. Just take me home so I can get cleaned up properly."

"You're not fine. You're not yourself."

My gaze snaps up and fixes on him. "You hardly know me."

"I know you well enough," he says, though the sting of my words is evident in the way his jaw tightens. "He's broken you."

He turns in his seat, facing forward, and starts the engine.

I shake my head. "No. He hasn't. He unlocked me." I turn my head away and watch the city begin to move past the window. The words taste like truth. But truth shouldn't feel so heavy in my mouth.

We arrive at my flat and Darius walks up the stairs with me, a heavy silence tethering me to him. I step inside and immediately flick off my shoes. I'm about to say good bye and close the door, when he steps past me, scoops up my shoes and wraps and arm around my waist, guiding me into the flat and kicking the door closed behind us.

"What are you doing?" I ask, my voice thick with fatigue.

"Making sure you're all right. Those were my instructions."

"Oh." Of course. He's following Thorne's orders. I give in and let him.

Darius deposits my shoes on the shoe rack in the bottom of my wardrobe and leads me into the bathroom. I'm not numb exactly, but drained. It's easier to let him do this than to resist. He starts the shower running. It's a large, glass-fronted cubicle filling one end of the narrow bathroom. The tiles are earthy tones and the lights set into the ceiling above it reflect off the glass and gleaming floor and walls.

The mirror above the sink catches my reflection and I falter. My makeup is smudged, black rings beneath my eyes, mascara trails like spilled ink. My hair is a wild tangle and my skin is deathly pale. I lock like a woman who's been wrecked.

Shame rises fast and brutal. My legs buckle, and I collapse onto the closed toilet seat, burying my face in my hands. A sob rips free before I can stop it.

Darius kneels in front of me and rests his hands on my thighs.

"Hey," he says gently. "You're safe. I've got you."

He says nothing more as I cry, as I let it all out—the confusion, the fear, the electric thrum of desire that still pulses beneath it all. He waits. Holds space.

When the sobs quiet to sniffles, he helps me to my feet with quiet care. Without a word, he undresses me and guides me into the hot stream. There's no leer, no lingering—just steady, simple help. Stripping off his shirt, he lathers my body wash between his hands and begins to wash me.

Gently. As though I'm something precious.

"Did he force you to do something you didn't want?" Darius asks, caution in his tone.

I shake my head. "No... I was willing. I let him. It was... intense. But it felt good, Darius. That's the worst part. I liked it."

He rinses my hair with cupped hands, his jaw tight, but his movements still tender.

"It's not the worst part," he murmurs. "Wanting to submit doesn't make you broken. I'm sorry I said that to you in the car."

I grip his arm. "But I am broken. Or I wouldn't crave someone like him."

He stills. "He's not all cruelty. You know that, don't

you? He sees something in you. Something he wants to protect, even if he doesn't know how."

I close my eyes. "It's not about protection. It's about surrender. With him... I don't have to think. I don't have to carry anything. I just... feel."

He nods once. "And with me?"

"With you, I feel safe. I feel seen. But maybe that's harder." My promise to Thorne echoes in my mind and guilt gnaws inside.

His throat bobs, but he doesn't argue.

When I'm clean and dry, he wraps me in a towel and leads me to the sofa. He disappears into the kitchen and returns with a glass of water and a hot cup of tea. Then he starts cooking. Scrambled eggs, wholemeal toast, some avocado. Something grounding. Something real.

I eat in silence, grateful. The food tastes better than anything I've had in days.

He doesn't press. He just watches. Waits.

When I'm finished, he helps me into a soft cotton dress and combs out my damp hair.

"You didn't have to do all this," I say quietly.

"I know."

A knock at the door interrupts us. Darius goes to answer it and I strain to hear, but the few words exchanged are soft and muffled. When he returns, he's holding a small package.

"It's from Thorne."

"Oh." I take it and gingerly unwrap the brown paper. It's the latest Ivy Halbrook novel. I've been meaning to pick up a copy. It's supposed to be scandalous. It's a surprisingly thoughtful and modern gift from Thorne. I'd have expected an antique first edition or something. I turn it over in my hands, examining the sprayed edges and foil print. I open it and find a note tucked inside.

*For Katrina,*

*To help you clear your busy head. But more importantly, because I listen when you speak.*

*T.*

My throat tightens.

Darius doesn't say a word.

But the look in his eyes says everything.

# CHAPTER ELEVEN

Thirst is quieter in the afternoons. The sharp glamour of evening hasn't set in yet, and the patrons here now are of an entirely different breed—solicitors in tailored suits murmuring over espresso, academics nursing black coffee while flipping through red-penned manuscripts, one woman laughing too loudly at her companion's joke, gold hoops catching the soft light from the chandelier overhead.

It's all so ordinary. Human. Real.

The contrast tugs at something in me.

I step through the doors and feel it instantly—that strange sense of dislocation. Like I'm walking through a dream I'm no longer part of. The rich scent of roasted coffee and orange peel, the soft scrape of chairs against the tiled floor, the hiss of the espresso machine—it should be comforting. But after last night, it all feels like theatre. A set. I half expect someone to pull back the curtain and reveal the world I now truly belong to:

shadows and silk and blood.

Lenora is behind the bar.

Of course she is.

She's speaking a member of the bar staff—a girl with short pink curls and a nose ring—but her gaze lifts the second I cross the threshold. Her expression doesn't change, but something cold flickers across it. She murmurs something to the girl, who nods and disappears through the back.

I make my way to the stairs that lead to the archive. I don't intend to stop, but Lenora intercepts me with feline grace, sliding out from behind the bar like smoke.

"You're back," she says coolly. "I wasn't sure you'd be… up for work today." The words are innocuous. The tone is not.

"I'm fine," I reply. A reflex.

Her eyes drift over me. "You look pale. Fragile." A pause. "But I suppose some people find that appealing."

Heat rises in my cheeks, but I don't take the bait.

"I'm just here to do my job."

"Of course you are. That's why Thorne hand picked you, isn't it? For your academic expertise." The sarcasm drips from every syllable.

I step past her, trying to maintain composure. She follows me with her eyes like a predator tracking prey.

"I'd be careful, Katrina," she adds lightly. "He loses interest quickly. It's not personal—he just tires of his toys."

That one hits the mark. My stomach clenches, but I keep walking.

"I'm not a toy," I say without turning back. "And I know why I'm here."

"Do you?" she calls after me. "Because the rest of us are still trying to figure that out."

I inhale slowly before looking back at her. "You're out of line."

Her eyes flash, but she reins herself in. "Enjoy the archive," she says, with mock cheer. "Let me know if you need anything. A glass of water. A safe word."

I don't respond. I just walk away, heels clicking on the marble floor. Her words settle behind me like ash.

Down in the cool hush of the archive, I let the silence wrap around me. But the memory of her voice—her smirk—clings like a bruise I can't rub away.

I bury myself in the records. For a time, I lose myself in parchment and ink, transcribing letters written by vampire hands centuries ago. Most are dry. Transactions, trade agreements, political manoeuvrings disguised in polite language. But I find a few gems—personal notes, scandalous rumours, veiled threats. I copy them carefully into my notes.

When my eyes begin to blur, I pack up and slip out the back, not willing to risk another encounter upstairs.

By the time I reach my flat, the late afternoon sun has mellowed to gold. I change into something soft and light, pour a glass of wine, and curl up with the book with my name on the first page. It opens easily now, the spine broken in and the pages familiar under my fingertips.

I start a new story. This one is more carnal than the

others. A woman torn between two lovers. Not in conflict—but in craving. Each man meets a different need. She doesn't want to choose.

My breath quickens. The words feel like they've been pulled from inside me. From my most private thoughts.

A knock at the door startles me. I nearly drop the book. I set it aside, heart fluttering, and go to the door. Darius stands on the threshold, dressed in dark jeans and a deep burgundy t-shirt that clings to his frame beneath a leather jacket. His hair is slightly mussed, his expression guarded. He looks quite different to the suited and booted man I'm used to.

"I came to check on you," he says. "Wanted to make sure you're... you."

I open the door wider. "Come in. I've got wine."

He hesitates for just a second, then steps inside. I close the door behind him, suddenly aware of how intimate the flat feels in the golden light. He hangs there in the entrance, his gaze scanning the living space. It takes me a second before I realise he can't go much further without stepping into direct sunlight.

"Oh! Of course." I hurry to the windows and draw the blinds and curtains, blocking out the sunset. "Now you can actually come in." I turn and smile to him.

He steps further into the flat and follows me to the kitchenette. I pour him a glass of red and lead him toward the sofa. He sits, back straight, his gaze flicking toward the book I left open on the armrest.

"That book," I say, following his gaze. "I found it here the day I arrived. Do you know anything about it?"

He shakes his head slowly. "No. I don't think so."

I lift it, running my fingers along the spine. "Every time I read it... I see myself. It's uncanny."

He takes a sip of wine, eyes still on the book. But he remains silent. This stoicism isn't like him and I feel the reluctance in him to be here, this close to me, testing Thorne's boundaries.

"Do you believe in fate?" I ask.

His gaze meets mine briefly before he looks away. "I believe in patterns. In intention. But I don't know about fate."

I lean back into the cushions. "The story I just read—it was..." I trail off, heat rushing to my cheeks. "Let's just say it was intense. It felt like my story. I can't explain it."

A charged silence stretches between us. His gaze lingers on my face, then drops to my mouth.

I take a long sip of wine to break the moment. My heart is racing again. I don't want to betray Thorne. But the way Darius cares for me has a pull on me that I can't ignore. I'm not entirely sure what the rules are that I'm supposed to be following. Thorne said he didn't mind my desire for Darius.

As if my every thought was laid bare for him, Darius puts his glass down on the coffee table and turns to face me.

"Kat, you have choices here. You're not owned by anyone." He places a hand on my knee and rubs his thumb slowly back and forth.

"Aren't I?" The question of what I've actually signed

up for rises from deep inside where it's been niggling at me for days.

Darius leans closer. Too close. Fuck. My heart is pounding.

"You have been claimed by one of the most powerful beings on this earth. He wants you. But he doesn't get to dictate how you feel, or what you want, or even what you do. You can choose your own path. I promise."

"And if I want you?" Our lips are almost touching. "As well as him?"

"Then you get to have us both. I won't flinch away from that." His lips press against mine with heat and hunger. I return the kiss and turn my body towards him, pulling him closer. I part my legs and he moves between my knees, smothering my body with his.

Fuck. I need him so badly. As cold as Thorne is, Darius is hot. As hard as Thorne is, Darius is soft. Not physically, oh no, there are no issues there and I feel the evidence pressing against my thigh. But in temperament, Darius is tender and caring. More so than any man I've known. He's not what I'd have expected from a vampire.

I press myself against him, yearning for more. But Darius peels his mouth from mine and pushes away from me.

"Are you sure this is what you want?"

"Yes," I say—breathless, impatient and needy. I grab his shirt and pull him back to me. Our mouths collide again and hands frantically tug at clothing until our naked bodies press together.

Darius thrusts into my already-wet entrance with a single, hungry stroke. My breath hitches and I arch my back.

"Fuck," he whispers at my ear as he begins to rock his hips.

I whimper in response and move with him, our bodies writhing together on the sofa. I cling to his back, my nails digging into his skin.

He groans at the scratch of my nails, hips thrusting harder in response. The couch creaks beneath us, a steady rhythm building that fills the room with heat and breath and low, delicious moans.

"God, you feel incredible," he murmurs against my neck, each word punctuated by a thrust that has me gasping.

I clutch at his shoulders, heels digging into the cushions for leverage. "Don't stop," I manage, though the pleasure is already edging toward overwhelming. "Don't you dare stop."

His mouth finds my breast, sucking and teasing until I'm crying out. One hand slips between us, fingers circling my clit with practised care, tipping me closer to the brink.

"You're so responsive," he breathes. "So ready. Like you've been waiting for this."

"I have," I gasp. "Darius—"

He silences my words with another kiss, slower this time. Not frantic. His movements slow too, drawing the moment out, letting the tension build again. I wrap my arms around his neck, anchoring myself to him as the world narrows to heat and rhythm and his whispered praises.

"That's it," he says as my body starts to tremble. "Let go for me."

And I do—shattering beneath him with a cry, my body clenching tight around him. He groans and thrusts harder, following me over the edge, hips stuttering as he spills inside me.

We lie tangled together, breathless, for long moments. My skin is slick with sweat, my limbs boneless. His hand strokes my side absently, and I feel that same unexpected comfort I always feel around him. Safe. Cherished.

But guilt threads through the afterglow, uninvited.

"I don't know how to make this work," I whisper.

He shifts just enough to look at me, brushing damp hair from my face. "You don't have to figure it all out tonight."

I nod, biting my lip.

Darius presses a kiss to my forehead. "But I meant what I said. You don't belong to anyone, Kat. You choose what—and who—you want."

I want to believe that. I want it to be simple. But nothing about this is.

And the night isn't over yet.

I shower again—this time alone. Steam curls

around me as hot water pounds against my skin, washing away the sweat and sex and uncertainty. I close my eyes and let it scald, chasing clarity I know won't come.

What the hell am I doing?

I dress slowly, each layer another piece of armour. A sleek crimson jumpsuit with a plunging neckline and a halter neck. My makeup is deliberate—bold red lips, dark smoky eyes to match the war inside me. I curl my hair into soft waves and pin one side back. Polished. Controlled. Even if I'm anything but.

In the mirror, I look powerful. Unbothered. Like a woman who knows exactly what she's doing.

I'm not sure I believe her.

Darius waits just inside the doorway when I emerge, his own clothes immaculate, his expression unreadable.

"Ready?" he asks.

No. "Yes."

We don't speak much on the way to Thirst. There's no need. The silence between us is heavy with what we've just done—and the knowledge that Thorne will know. He always does.

As we approach the door, Darius casts me a sideways glance. "Whatever happens tonight... I'm with you."

I nod, spine straightening as we step into the warm, golden glow of Thirst.

Time to face the music.

Thirst hums with the buzz of evening. The lighting

is low and golden, casting everyone in soft shadows and false warmth. The scent of citrus and spice hangs in the air. I walk beside Darius, our steps in sync. My jumpsuit hugs my frame like second skin, the deep V-neckline brushing scandalous territory. I feel his gaze flick toward me more than once, though he says nothing.

As we move through the upstairs bar, Darius places a hand at the small of my back, guiding me through the crowd. It's a light touch, easily dismissed, but my skin tingles beneath it. It's subtle, but it says everything. I glance up at him and smile.

And that's when I feel it—the prickle at the back of my neck. I turn my head just enough to see her.

Lenora.

Perched at the far end of the bar, a glass of crimson liquid in one hand, her elbow resting elegantly on the bar. Her lips are pressed into a tight, unreadable line, but her eyes are all ice and daggers. Fixed. On. Me.

She saw.

I look away quickly, heat rising in my cheeks despite my efforts to appear unbothered. My body hums with awareness, not just from Darius's proximity, but from the weight of Lenora's gaze. She's watching. Measuring. And I don't doubt she'll report every detail.

I lean into Darius, just slightly, as we enter the corridor to the lift down to the private floor below.

If this is a game, then I've just made my next move.

# CHAPTER TWELVE

The lower level of Thirst is quieter than usual when Darius and I enter, the steady thrum of music muted, the shadows deeper. Candles flicker in red glasses on low tables, throwing glints of gold across polished wood and black velvet.

We weave through clusters of patrons lounging in conversation, their low murmurs blending with the soft clink of crystal. A couple dressed in matching silk shares a blood-slicked kiss in the far corner. Another pair disappears behind a curtain, laughter trailing in their wake.

Darius walks just half a step behind me, his presence close but not possessive. We don't touch. Not here. Not now. Our hands remain at our sides, our expressions neutral. But my skin tingles with the memory of his touch, of everything we shared this evening.

I scan the room, but Thorne isn't in his throne and

there's no sign of him anywhere else.

"We're early," I say softly, all too aware of the quiet.

"Let's get a drink." Darius indicates the bar and we move over to it. The bartender—a young man with striking blond hair and dark eyes—nods at Darius with silent recognition. We each order something. Wine for me. Blood-spiked whiskey for him.

As the drinks are placed in front of us, our hands brush beneath the bar. Not clumsily, not accidentally—deliberately. Hidden from view, our fingers curl together for the briefest of seconds. My breath catches.

He doesn't look at me. Just lifts his glass and takes a sip, as if nothing has happened.

I press my lips together to conceal a smile and take a sip of my wine. I dare to shift my weight so that my hip bumps against his. He doesn't move away. This feels more dangerous than anything else I've done since I entered this world. My heart skips a beat and my cheeks blaze with heat.

As we sip our drinks and share secret touches, the bar grows steadily busier with new arrivals. The volume picks up as vampires and their thralls strike up conversations, drink, feed. I try not to stare at the couple at the other end of the bar who are locked in a tight embrace, the female vampire latched onto the human man's neck.

We've probably been at the bar for twenty minutes, barely exchanging a word, when a hush sweeps through the room.

I glance toward the lift and feel it—like the air itself takes a step back.

Thorne has arrived.

He cuts a striking figure as always, dressed in black on black, his silk waistcoat embroidered with threads so dark they glimmer like oil in candlelight. His silver hair loose and flowing down his back. An entourage trails behind him—three vampires I recognise, each dressed with care and carrying an aura of lethal grace. And just behind them, smiling like she owns the room, is Lenora.

She clocks me instantly and lifts her chin, smug satisfaction curling her lips.

But Thorne... doesn't look pleased.

His eyes sweep the room like a storm front rolling in. He speaks to no one at first, simply crosses the floor with slow, predatory purpose. One of his companions peels off to join a group near the fireplace. Another disappears behind a velvet curtain. Lenora lingers close to Thorne's elbow, her posture suggesting possession.

He stops to murmur something to a sharply dressed couple seated near his throne. Offers a ghost of a smile to a server. Makes a slow, deliberate circuit of the lounge.

All without looking at me.

The tension coils tighter with each step he takes.

I sip my wine, throat dry.

Darius stays close, his presence grounding me, but even he looks wary now. We both know this can't last. That he will come.

And when Thorne finally turns and walks toward us—eyes sharp, mouth tight—it's not with welcome in his gaze.

It's with malice.

Thorne halts a few steps from us, his expression unreadable. He doesn't look at me. Doesn't even acknowledge me. His gaze is fixed solely on Darius.

"Walk with me," he says.

Darius inclines his head in silent deference and follows as Thorne strides towards the centre of the lounge the people parting for him. I remain frozen in place, the stem of my wineglass slippery in my fingers. From across the room, Lenora watches with thinly veiled glee.

Thorne draws Darius to his side, an arm wrapped around Darius's shoulders, pinning him close. His voice is low and inaudible beneath the ambient hum of the bar, but his posture speaks volumes. There's a rigidity in the line of his shoulders, a quiet wrath that coils beneath the surface.

Darius listens, says nothing.

Then, without warning, Thorne turns back toward me.

His gaze is a blade.

He lifts one elegant hand and crooks a finger.

"Come," he says in a voice that carries cleanly over the music and hum of our audience.

I obey, leaving my almost empty glass on the bar.

I don't dare catch Darius's eye as the three of us walk together through the thickening crowd, past tables and alcoves and velvet-covered booths, until we reach Thorne's seat. It isn't the dungeon's monstrous throne, but it's no less imposing—high-backed, carved from dark wood, its arms wide enough to command distance, its seat just large enough for two.

Thorne sits and extends a hand.

I take it.

He draws me to him and guides me down onto the seat—no, onto him—so that I'm perched between his legs, my back pressed against his chest. My pulse kicks up as his arm wraps around my chest, keeping me there, tethered and displayed. A murmur ripples through the room, subtle as smoke.

Thorne leans in, his lips brushing my ear. "You've made quite the impression this evening."

I swallow hard. "I didn't mean—"

His hand moves slowly, deliberately, to sweep my hair off my left shoulder.

"No," he murmurs, "you didn't mean to."

His cool lips press against the curve of my neck, sending a shiver down my spine. He lays a trail of soft kisses on my skin. I feel almost every eye in the place on us. On me. Exposed like this. I hold my breath. I know what's coming.

His fangs pierce me with effortless precision.

Pain blooms and vanishes in an instant, replaced by heat. Pleasure. My body goes still, then pliant. My eyes flutter shut—but only for a moment. When they open, I find Darius standing sentinel just a few feet from us. Watching. His expression is carved from stone, but I can feel the tension in his frame. The way his hands curl into fists at his sides. He's barely holding it together.

And I—God help me—I'm on fire.

Thorne drinks with the slow indulgence of a connoisseur. His right hand lays firmly against my chest above the swell of my breasts, cool against my skin. His left hand grips my hip. Every draw of his mouth sends another rush of sensation down my spine, settling between my legs. His arousal presses against my back.

I grip the arms of the chair, unsure whether to pull away or press closer.

Finally, he withdraws.

The bite seals behind his lips like it was never there. He presses a kiss to the wound, and then another, higher on my neck, more tender than I expect.

His voice is low, meant only for me.

"You taste of secrets, my dear. And disobedience."

My pulse stutters.

"I wonder," he continues, brushing his lips against my cheek, "how long you'll make me chase you." He straightens in the chair, his eyes once again scanning the lounge, every inch the monarch at court. But his grip on me doesn't ease.

And I know this performance has only just begun.

Darius's eyes are narrowed, his jaw tight, but he doesn't look away even though he looks as though it's taking every ounce of effort to stay where he stands.

I wonder if Thorne is controlling him, making him watch. The slightest tightening of his grip on me tells me I'm right and that he's inside my head too.

*You both need to learn that there are consequences for your actions, my dear.*

Thorne rises beneath me, lifting me effortlessly as

he stands, then sets me on my feet beside him. "Come," he says, his voice like silk drawn over steel. Darius follows without a word as Thorne leads us through the lounge.

We don't head toward the lift or the private chambers. Instead, we move to one of the shadowed alcoves near the back of the lounge—a space half-secluded by a thick velvet curtain. It's not soundproof. Not locked. Just hidden from direct view.

He sweeps the curtain aside with a flick of his fingers and gestures for us to enter.

Inside, the lighting is low and sensual, gold from a single candle dancing across the deep garnet upholstery of a plush chaise. The table beside it bears an open bottle of blood-infused wine, two glasses—untouched. The sound of conversation, laughter, and clinking glasses hums just beyond the curtain, a reminder that this is not entirely private.

That's the point, isn't it?

Thorne turns to face us, his gaze sharp, predatory. "Remove your clothing," he says, addressing me.

My pulse jumps, but I obey, unfastening the jumpsuit and letting it slide down my body. I step out of it wearing just black, lacy underwear. The cool air kisses my skin, and I feel Darius's gaze burn across every inch of me. His hands twitch at his sides.

"All of it," Thorne commands. I hold his gaze as I unhook my strapless bra. Likewise as I tug the underwear down my legs. I stand there in just my killer black heels as Thorne drinks me in and Darius tries not to look at me. Self-conscious heat rises up my neck. The noise of the bar is too loud, too close.

Thorne steps in behind me, his hands trailing down my sides, possessive and deliberate. "Do you feel him watching?" he whispers, lips brushing the shell of my ear.

I nod. My sights set on Darius standing by the curtain.

"Good. Let him see what belongs to me."

His hand slides between my thighs and a slender finger slips inside me, and I bite back a gasp. Darius's fists clench. His jaw flexes. He does not look away.

Thorne removes his finger and brings it to his lips. He sucks my slick arousal off it with relish and utters a deep, sensual moan. He slowly undresses himself as I stand there, naked, vulnerable. I catch Darius's eye and we hold the contact for just a second. Long enough to see the longing and regret in his eyes.

The elder vampire moves me to the chaise and positions me on all fours, my hands on the armrest at one end. Heat and anticipation rush through my body making my skin tingle. And yet I hate what this is doing to Darius. I feel his frustration building through our bond. Rage mingled with desire.

Thorne positions himself behind me, one foot on the chaise beside me, the other rooted to the stone floor. His hands caress my hips and back as the head of his cock presses against my entrance.

"Look at him, my dear." Thorne instructs.

I turn my head to look at Darius, still standing like a statue by the curtain, his expression a careful mask—

until Thorne speaks again.

"Hold her gaze, Darius. Let her see what she does to you."

And so he does. His eyes lock with mine, full of longing, of jealousy, of want. And something deeper. Something dangerous.

Thorne eases himself into my dripping pussy and a groan rushes from my mouth. I want to apologise to Darius. I want him to know how much he means to me. But I also need Thorne inside me like I need oxygen. Confusion swells in me as he moves in me. A cry of desperation bubbles out of me and Darius's expression becomes pained.

"This should hurt you both," Thorne says, his voice low and dangerous. He takes long, deep thrusts of his hips, driving his point deep inside me. "I will not tolerate the two of you carrying on behind my back. Katrina," he grips my hips hard, digging his fingers into the flesh. "You are mine to pleasure and to feed from. I thought you understood that."

"She's not your slave," Darius says through gritted teeth.

"No," Thorne says, punctuating his word with a hard thrust of his hips. I cry bursts out of me. "She chose this. She gave herself to me."

"After I'd already claimed her," Darius says, taking half a step towards us.

"I'm not livestock," I hiss, half way to climaxing but maddeningly excluded from this debate. "Fuck. I want you both, dammit. I want you both. Oh God!" Thorne is pumping away at me, gripping my hips hard enough to draw blood. My orgasm rushes up through me and I doubt every word I've ever said about feminism, agency, choice. In this moment, as I come under this ancient monster who desires me more than any other, I will submit, willingly. My eyes close as I cry out with intense pleasure.

Thorne grabs a handful of my long hair and yanks me hard, pulling me up and slamming my back against his chest even as he continues to fuck me. When he bites, it's without warning. Sharp and precise, the pleasure immediate, drowning thought. My body arches into him, hips shifting involuntarily.

And still, I stare at Darius.

Still, he watches.

And in the strength of Thorne's bite and the flare of Darius's nostrils, I know: this isn't punishment.

It's power.

And I am the weapon they're both wielding.

## CHAPTER THIRTEEN

Thorne's mouth leaves my neck, and the sudden absence is a shock—cold air rushing in where there had been nothing but heat and hunger. My knees buckle, and I fold onto the chaise, my palms sinking into the plush upholstery as the room tilts faintly around me. My pulse thunders weakly in my ears, every beat slower than it should be.

I barely register Darius moving until he's already across the alcove, fury carved into every line of him.

"Bastard—"

Thorne is faster. Always faster. One moment Darius is lunging, the next his back slams against the wall hard enough to rattle the candle on the table. Thorne's hand is a vice at his throat, pinning him like a moth beneath glass.

The elder vampire's snarl is low and cold, reverberating in the marrow of my bones. "Do you forget what you are, fledgling? Who made you? Who gave you every scrap of power you possess?"

Darius's eyes blaze with defiance. "She's not—"

"She is mine," Thorne cuts in, the words precise, final. "My claim takes precedence. Always. You will remember your place." He leans in, his voice dropping to a whisper edged in steel. "And if you cannot accept that, you will lose far more than her."

I want to tell them to stop. To make them both listen. But my body feels heavy, boneless, as though he's drained not just my blood but my strength to resist. I can only watch, breath shallow, the taste of copper and him still thick on my tongue.

Thorne releases Darius abruptly, stepping back with the unhurried grace of a predator who knows there's no threat worth fearing. Darius stays against the wall, chest heaving, jaw tight.

Without looking at him again, Thorne retrieves his discarded clothing and dresses with swift, efficient movements. His hands are steady, his expression once more smoothed into regal composure, as though the moment of violence never happened.

When he's finished, he turns to me. His cool palm brushes my temple, then he bends, pressing a single kiss to my forehead—a strangely intimate gesture that makes my heart ache and my stomach twist.

"Rest, my dear," he murmurs. "You will need it."

Then he's gone, sweeping aside the curtain and vanishing into the hum of the lounge beyond.

Darius is at my side instantly, crouching beside the chaise. "Kat." His voice is softer now, the anger banked but still glowing beneath the surface. "You all right?"

I nod, though the movement feels sluggish. "Just... tired."

He helps me to sit up and quickly locates my discarded jumpsuit, carefully helping me shimmy back into it. I've never felt so vulnerable, exposed, raw. To be treated so cruelly and yet be desired so intensely is a dizzying cocktail of emotions.

Darius tucks a heavy blanket around my shoulders.

"I'll send food and water. You'll feel steadier soon."

I catch his wrist before he can rise. "Stay."

His gaze flicks to the curtain, his jaw tightening. "I can't. He's calling me." There's no mistaking the bitterness in his voice—or the invisible pull dragging him toward his master. He leans in, his hand warm against my cheek. "I'll come back as soon as I can."

Then he's gone, the velvet curtain swaying shut behind him.

I lie still, listening to the muffled voices beyond, the lingering thrum of music. The blanket is warm but does little to ease the chill inside me. I'm not sure how long I wait before the curtain parts again.

It's not Darius.

Lenora steps inside, her heels clicking softly on the stone floor. She takes in the scene—the half-fastened jumpsuit, the blanket around my shoulders, the paleness of my skin—with a slow, simmering glare.

"Well," she says, the sweetness in her voice as fake as spun sugar. "Break the rules and you get him all to yourself. How... fortunate for you."

Her mouth twists, something bitter sparking in her eyes. "Some of us wait years for the honour, and you stumble into it like a spoiled child handed a crown."

She lets her gaze sweep over me, lingering on my throat, my bare collarbone, the marks Thorne left behind. "You should be on your knees begging forgiveness, not lying there looking like you've just been... satisfied."

The contempt in her tone is colder than the stone floor under my bare feet.

Lenora steps closer, her expression softening by an almost imperceptible degree. "You're trembling," she says, voice low. "You need air. Come on—let's get you out of here before you faint in front of everyone."

I blink at her, the suggestion almost reasonable through the haze of exhaustion and the steady ache where Thorne's fangs pierced me. My limbs feel like they belong to someone else—heavy, slow, unresponsive.

"Come on," she urges, slipping an arm under mine and pulling me to my feet. My knees buckle but she keeps me upright with surprising strength. "That's it. Lean on me."

I let her guide me through the velvet curtain and into the lounge. The crowd thins as we move, the murmur of conversation dimming under the persistent thud of my heartbeat in my ears. A few patrons glance our way, eyes curious or knowing, but no one intervenes. No Darius. No Thorne.

The air smells faintly of spiced wine and candle wax, but my senses feel muted, dulled by the blood loss and whatever cocktail of adrenaline and pleasure is still coursing through me. My head lolls once against her shoulder before I force it upright again.

We reach a narrow doorway at the back, and the moment it closes behind us, the softness in her grip vanishes.

Her fingers dig into my arm.

The corridor is dim and smells of damp stone and something faintly metallic—rust, or blood. Shadows stretch across the walls as we pass under flickering sconces.

"Lenora—" My voice is a rasp.

"Save it," she snaps, her tone sharp enough to cut. "You've had enough indulgence for one night."

I try to pull back, but my legs are barely holding me. She drags me along, my bare feet scraping against the uneven floor, each jolt sending a throb of pain up my calves. My chest tightens with the growing certainty that this is wrong.

We round a corner into a tunnel so narrow the walls graze my bare arms. The air grows colder, sharper. My breath comes in shallow bursts.

"Where are we—"

"Quiet."

The world tilts. My knees give out completely, and the last thing I feel is the rough bite of stone against my shoulder before everything goes black.

Rain wakes me.

Cold, insistent drops spatter against my cheeks, slicking my hair to my face. My lashes clump together, and when I force them open, the world is a blur of grey and shadow. The stone at my back is slick, its chill seeping into my bones.

I try to move and find my wrists bound high above my head, the rope rough and unyielding, cutting into my skin when I twist. My shoulders ache. My feet slip on the wet flagstones.

Lenora's voice cuts through the darkness. She's pacing a few feet away, muttering under her breath—sharp fragments of words spilling out in a rhythm of contempt. "Pathetic... undeserving... handed everything..." Her heels click and skid slightly on the rain-slick ground, her movements erratic.

A flash of lightning throws the courtyard into stark relief, and my stomach twists. I know this place. The castle. By day, it would be crawling with tourists—cameras clicking, children chasing each other over the cobbles. But now, it's just me, the empty expanse, and the cold rain pouring from a sky split with thunder.

The scent of wet stone and moss mixes with something metallic—iron from the bindings, or the blood still drying at my neck. My teeth chatter, my knees threaten to buckle, and the rope jerks taut each time I sag forward.

Lenora turns to me, her eyes bright with a feverish light. "He should have punished you. He should have broken you." Her voice drops to a venomous hiss. "Instead, he gave you what I've waited years for. And you... don't... even... appreciate it."

Each word feels like a nail driven into the wall behind me, holding me there as surely as the ropes.

Lenora stops pacing and just stares at me, rain streaming down her face, plastering her auburn hair against her temples. The wet only makes her beauty sharper, crueller—like a blade fresh from the whetstone.

"You think you've been chosen," she says, her voice low, intimate. "That you've done something special to earn his attention." She takes a step closer, the sound of her heels dull on the slick stone. "Do you have any idea how many nights I've been in that room? How many times I've bled for him? Fed him. Pleased him. Waited for him to see me?"

Her lip curls, and she laughs—too high, too thin to be amusement. "And then you arrive. Soft little scholar with your wide eyes and your clever questions. You stumble into this world, disobey him, flaunt another man right under his nose—and what does he do? He fucks you in front of the one you betrayed him with."

The word fucks lands like a slap, hot and deliberate.

Her steps quicken. She circles me now, her shadow passing over my bound form, her perfume mingling with the wet stone and iron. "He was supposed to punish you and reward me. This should have been my night." She spits the last word, and I feel the flecks of it on my cheek, mingled with rain.

She's close enough that her breath brushes my lips. "You don't understand the game you're playing, Katrina. You've already lost. You just don't know it yet."

Her fingers lift to my neck, tracing the fresh bite

mark with deceptive gentleness. My breath catches—half from the touch, half from the icy current of fear crawling down my spine.

Lenora's eyes glint in the dim light. "He might've marked you tonight, but I can unmake that just as easily. When I'm done with you, he won't see a consort. He'll see a corpse."

She steps back suddenly, as though the thought excites her. Her hands tremble—not from the cold, but from the charge of some wild, festering hunger. "No one will question me. You'll be found here, some tragic accident, another foolish human who thought she could keep up with our world." She begins pacing again. Her voice sharpens into something like glee. "And then? Then I'll comfort him. I'll remind him of the woman who never faltered. Who earned her place at his side."

Lightning flashes again, white and searing. For an instant, her face is all edges, all hate, her mouth twisted into something almost feral.

"He won't hear a cross word about you, you know? He values you, Lenora. You don't have to do this." I pull at the ropes, the coarse fibres biting into my wrists, panic fizzing hot in my veins—but the more I struggle, the tighter they seem to grip. The rain pours harder now, soaking me through, blurring the edges of my vision.

Lenora tilts her head, watching me like a cat studying a bird with a broken wing. "Struggle all you like," she murmurs. "It'll warm you up before the end."

She stalks over to me and clamps a hand around my throat.

"You know what the difference is between us?" she asks, and there's a tremor in her voice that has nothing to do with the cold. "You still think you matter to him. That this is... love." She gives a little laugh, sharp and hollow. "Thorne doesn't love. He claims. He consumes. And when he's done, he discards."

Her fingers tighten until her nails press into my skin, the sting dulled by the numbing chill of the rain. "I've seen it before. I've watched others fall, thinking they were chosen. And now it's you. His latest plaything. You don't get to take my place just because he's bored."

She releases my neck in one fluid motion and starts pacing again, muttering under her breath. The words drift and tangle, fragments of old grievances and jealous oaths. "Years... always at his side... she walks in... nothing..."

Another flash of lightning throws her shadow long across the courtyard wall, a monstrous silhouette.

When she turns back to me, her expression has smoothed into something eerily calm, but her eyes blaze. "You don't deserve what you've been given. But don't worry." She reaches behind her, and the faint metallic scrape of a blade being drawn cuts through the rain. "I'll make it quick."

The sight of the knife jolts me like a plunge into ice water. It's not ornate or ceremonial—just a simple, wickedly sharp blade, the kind meant to do a job efficiently.

My pulse slams in my ears. I try to speak, but my voice is raw, thin. "He'll know."

"Oh, yes, he'll know," she says, stepping close, the

knife glinting as it catches a shred of moonlight. "And maybe he'll be angry for a night, maybe two. But then? Then he'll see what I've done for him. For us."

She brings the blade up—not to my throat, but to my cheek, tracing the curve of my jaw with the flat of it. The metal is cold enough to burn. "You're nothing but a reminder that he can be stolen from. And I'm going to take that reminder away."

Rain patters harder on the flagstones, masking the sound of my quickening breath. My wrists twist uselessly against the ropes, fibres cutting deep. The damp fabric of her sleeves clings to her arms, carrying the sharp scent of rain and the faint, metallic bite of steel.

Lenora smiles faintly, almost wistfully, and for a moment she looks like someone remembering a dream. Then the smile fades, her grip on the knife tightening. "Say goodbye, Katrina."

The blade presses to my throat. Desperation flares, hot and bright, and I yank my left hand with everything I have. The rope bites, snaps—and I'm free enough to lash out. My palm strikes her wrist, knocking the knife wide just as a dark shape drops from above.

Thorne lands beside me in a spray of rain, the impact rattling the iron ring still holding my right wrist. Before Lenora can recover from my strike, he has her pinned to the wall, her feet barely touching the ground. His hand closes around her throat like an iron collar.

"You dare," he says, voice low and deadly, "to touch what is mine?"

Lenora claws at his wrist, shaking her head, but

Thorne doesn't relent. "After everything I've given you. Years of loyalty. Of protection. And you repay me with this?" His other hand wrenches the knife from her grip. It clatters to the ground between us.

"You think I wouldn't smell your jealousy on you the moment I walked into the lounge?" His lips peel back from his teeth. "You've been circling her like a vulture, waiting for me to falter. You forget yourself, Lenora. I do not share. I do not forgive."

Her mouth opens—maybe to beg, maybe to curse—but the words never come. Thorne's fangs punch into her throat with brutal precision. The sound is obscene, a wet tearing beneath the hammer of the rain. She kicks once, twice, and then goes slack in his grip.

He drinks long and deep and when he pulls back, her body hangs lifeless from his hand. He lets her drop in an unceremonious heap on the wet stone.

Darius appears at my side, cutting the rest of my bonds, his touch urgent but gentle. My arm is still trembling from the effort of that single blow, my heart racing with shock and adrenaline.

Thorne wipes the back of his hand across his mouth, eyes glittering in the rain as they land on me.

"Next time," he says, as if Lenora's corpse isn't cooling at our feet, "don't wait until the blade is at your throat."

# CHAPTER FOURTEEN

The rain hasn't stopped by the time we reach my flat. Darius unlocks the door with a key I didn't know he had, and Thorne follows us inside without ceremony, his long coat dripping onto the polished floorboards like a slow, elegant invasion.

The familiar scent of my place—warm vanilla and old books—wraps around me as soon as I step in, but tonight it feels almost alien. I make it as far as the sofa before gravity wins, sinking into the cushions with a sigh that could probably double as a confession.

Darius crouches in front of me, brushing damp strands from my face. "You should change into something dry before you get a chill."

"She's exhausted," Thorne says from behind him, voice smooth but edged. "The only thing she should be doing is sitting still."

Darius glances over his shoulder. "And she'll sit still after she changes."

"She'll sit still now." Thorne strides into the kitchen like he owns it—which, annoyingly, he does.

There's a clink of glassware, the pop of a cork, and then Darius's voice drifting after him: "You're not giving her that."

"It's fortified with herbs," Thorne replies smoothly. "A tonic older than both of us. Restorative."

"She needs warmth, not some medieval hangover cure."

"I don't make tea."

"It's boiling water and pouring it into in a mug, Thorne. Not exactly sorcery."

A beat of silence. Then a clipped "Fine."

I press my lips together to stifle a laugh.

When they return, Darius is holding a steaming mug of Lady Grey tea, and Thorne is carrying a heavy glass tumbler of something the colour of burnished amber. The tea smells like comfort. The other drink smells like a forest after rain, sharp and resinous.

They set them both on the coffee table like rival champions.

"Tea," Darius says firmly.

"Tonic," Thorne counters, as though the outcome is inevitable.

I manage a tired smile. "You realise you sound like an old married couple, right?"

Thorne's mouth curves faintly. Darius just mutters, "Not in this lifetime."

"You'll drink both," Thorne says, settling into the

armchair opposite with the poise of a king displaced from his throne. "One for your warmth, one for your strength."

It's the most jarring sight I've had since I arrived in Edinburgh. Which is saying something. This ancient vampire lord sitting in a squashy armchair in my cosy but modern flat. His silver hair hangs in wet twists like rope over his shoulders and blood still stains his pale lips. He doesn't seem to notice—or care—but his gaze remains fixed on me, sharp as cut glass even in this absurdly domestic setting.

Darius sits himself on the sturdy, wooden coffee table beside the two drinks, close enough that his presence feels like a shield. He waits until I've sipped the tea before he speaks.

"You should rest. Properly. At least for a day or two."

"She'll do as she's told," Thorne says, but without the bite I expect. He studies me for a moment longer, then leans back into the chair. "Though perhaps... your methods have merit, fledgling."

Darius's brow ticks up. "Is that your way of saying I'm right?"

Thorne's lips curl faintly. "It's my way of saying I'll permit your interference—if it keeps her alive."

The exchange hangs between them, barbed but not hostile. And strangely... I feel seen in it. I set the mug down, the heat still lingering in my hands.

"Both of you... thank you. For getting me out of there." My voice catches, the memory of Lenora's blade still a phantom at my throat. "If you hadn't..."

Darius shakes his head. "Don't think about that."

Thorne's expression doesn't soften, but his tone does. "Lenora sealed her fate the moment she touched you. I won't tolerate threats to what is mine."

It's possessive, yes—but there's something else under it. Something quieter.

I meet his eyes, unsure if I should push. "She would have killed me."

"Yes," he says simply. "Which is why she is gone."

Darius glances at him, some unspoken understanding passing between them. Then he rises, fetching the blanket draped over the back of the armchair and tucking it around me with a gentleness that makes my throat ache.

For a moment, the three of us sit in a silence that isn't uncomfortable. Rain taps steadily at the windows. The steam from my tea curls into the warm air. And I feel, for the first time since all this began, something dangerously close to safe.

Thorne is the one to break the quiet. "Lenora's absence will raise questions."

"Not from the human authorities," Darius says without looking at him. "I've already sent word. It'll be handled."

Thorne inclines his head, satisfied. "Good. The fewer mortal eyes on our affairs, the better." His gaze returns to me. "You don't need the details. Only that it won't touch you."

I let out a slow breath. "I'm not sure I want to know the details."

"Wise," Thorne says, rising to his feet with liquid grace. He looks so out of place here, in my small, lived-in flat, as though the shadows should cling to him and the air should be colder.

Darius straightens too, though he stays beside me. "She'll rest," he says firmly. "And I'll be here to make sure of it."

Something flickers in Thorne's eyes—territorial, maybe, or simply reluctant concession. "See that you do," he murmurs. Then, after a beat, "And don't let her wander into trouble before she's ready to stand again."

"I'm sitting right here, you know," I mutter, though my voice is too tired to sound convincing.

Thorne's lips curve faintly. "Yes, my dear. You are." He steps closer, and for a moment I think he might touch me, but instead he just studies me—like a jeweller checking for flaws—before turning away. Thorne's gaze drifts over the room, taking in the bookshelves, the low lamplight, the scattered remnants of my mortal life. His hand settles on the end table beside me, fingers brushing the worn leather cover of the book I found here.

He picks it up idly, turning it over in one elegant hand. "Yours?"

"No," I say slowly, watching him. "It was here when I arrived. Did you put it here?"

A faint crease forms between his brows. "No."

Something unsettles in my chest. "Have you been in the flat since I moved in? At night, maybe?" My voice drops, quieter. "While I was asleep?" The memory of those dreams—of a shadow at the foot of my bed—

prickles along my spine.

His eyes meet mine, steady, unblinking. "No." There's no shift in his voice, no tell-tale flicker in his expression. If he's lying, he's better at it than anyone I've ever met.

He flips the book open, glances at a page or two, then raises an eyebrow at whatever he sees. "Interesting taste in reading material." He lets it fall shut and drops it back onto the table as if it's of no consequence at all.

But my gaze lingers on it. The unease sharpens into something more deliberate, a thought I don't quite want to chase yet: maybe this isn't just a book. Maybe it's something else entirely.

"Have you read the book I gifted to you yet?" Thorne asks, an edge of a demand in his query.

"Not yet," I say with half a smile. "I haven't had much time. But I'll read it while I recover from all of this." I wave a hand and Thorne nods once, his lips pressed into a thin line. He straightens, the moment gone.

"Rest," he says simply, as if closing the matter. He stalks towards the door and it closes behind him with a whisper of rain-cooled air, and the flat seems to exhale.

Darius's gaze lingers on the door for a moment, head tilted as if listening to be certain Thorne is gone. When he finally turns to face me, the tension in his shoulders eases.

"How are you feeling?" he asks.

"Tired. Shaky." I manage a faint smile. "But alive. Thanks to you. And him."

His mouth curves, but it's shadowed by something more serious. "You'd have been fine without me."

I shake my head. "No. I wouldn't have. You were there when I needed you. Twice over, tonight."

He sits beside me on the sofa, close enough that our knees touch. The faint warmth of him seeps into me, settling the last of my shivers. He takes my hand, his thumb brushing idly over the back of it, as if grounding himself as much as me.

"I hated seeing him touch you like that," he admits quietly. "But I couldn't... I had to step in when it really mattered. That's what I'm here for, Kat. To keep you safe. Even from him, if I have to."

Something twists warmly in my chest. I lean into him, resting my head against his shoulder. "I know. And I'm grateful for it. For you."

He huffs a soft laugh, tilting his head to rest against mine. "You've had a hell of a night. You should sleep. I'll stay as long as you want me to."

"Just for a while," I murmur. "Until I know the walls aren't going to close in."

His arm comes around me then, drawing me in, steady and certain. And for the first time since Lenora dragged me into the rain, I feel safe enough to let my eyes close.

Darius stays with me all night, holding me, moving me to the bed at some point and removing my wet clothes. I wake in the dark with his firm body pressed against my back, spooning me and holding me securely in his arms. I drift back to sleep for a time and wake again being gently stroked along my hip and side, his erection pressing between my thighs. With a sleepy whimper of need, I adjust my hips and lift my leg to allow him in.

"Are you sure?" he whispers at me ear.

"Yes," I murmur back.

Without a word, he eases inside me. I'm not that wet, so his cock sticks slightly part way in but I nudge my hips back and take him in deeper with a groan of satisfaction.

We rock slowly together, his arms around me and one hand softly kneading one of my breasts. I drape my free hand over his hip and move with him, whimpering softly at the sensation of his dick moving in me.

"Is this how it will be?" I ask after a while, my voice thick with sleep. "Do I get to keep you both?"

"I think so," he says, still gently spooning me. "I will always care for you. Regardless of anyone else."

Sleepily, we stay like that for hours, moving slowly. There's no explosion, just tenderness. The safety of his arms is intoxicating. I could live out the rest of my days this way. And I intend to.

# CHAPTER FIFTEEN

Three days later, I return to Thirst.

The first time I walked through these doors, the air had been thick with danger, my every step dogged by suspicion. Tonight, it feels different. Warmer.

A few patrons lift their glasses to me in silent greeting as I pass. Others nod or offer small smiles. The edge of hostility that once hummed just beneath the surface is gone—or at least, blunted.

Even the atmosphere feels lighter. The new manager, a broad-shouldered vampire named Callen with dark skin and a voice like velvet, moves between customers at the bar with easy charm. He greets me like an old friend, pressing a glass of wine into my hand before I've even asked. "Good to have you back, Katrina."

I thank him, feeling a surprising wash of belonging as I head towards the far side of the room.

Whispers swirl in pockets around the lounge.

Lenora's name is on more than one tongue, but no one seems to know the truth. The stories vary—she's left the city, she's gone to serve another master, she was seen boarding a midnight train. None of them are right, but all of them are far safer than what really happened.

At the far end of the room, Thorne's throne awaits. He sits already, black-clad and severe, his expression carved from the same stone as the wall behind him. The conversations around us quieten as I approach, but his eyes soften—just a fraction—when they meet mine.

"Katrina." My name in his voice is a summons and a welcome all at once. He extends a hand, and I place mine in it, allowing him to guide me into the seat beside his. His fingers brush my wrist as he releases me, a brief, private touch that feels almost like a secret.

On my other side, Darius is already seated. Without hesitation, he rests a hand on my thigh, his thumb stroking a lazy pattern through the fabric of my dress. It's not hidden, not subtle, and it earns us a few curious glances. But no one speaks against it—not with Thorne sitting in silent approval a breath away.

The three of us make a strange tableau. I can feel the weight of eyes on us, the questions building behind polite silence. But Thorne reclines with the unshakable ease of a ruler whose authority is unquestioned, and so no one dares to ask.

For the first time, I feel like I'm not just surviving here. I'm part of something—dangerous, yes, but mine.

Late into the evening, Thorne rises without a word and a mere glance in my direction lifts me to my feet. Darius too. We follow him, the remaining vampires and their companions parting for us as we weave through the lounge, between tables and chairs, and out into the corridor. We walk in silence and I recognise the route. We climb the stairs and emerge in Thorne's private chambers.

He leads us into his bedroom and Darius and I file inside. Thorne follows us and closes the heavy, wooden door firmly behind him.

"I have never shared a thrall before," he says, his voice low and dangerous. "I make no promises that this will be easy. But, my darling Katrina, you have opened my mind."

He moves over to me, almost gliding across the stone floor. He gently unzips my dress and slips it down my body. My breath hitches.

Darius moves closer and wraps a possessive hand around my waist.

"We can't feed on her again yet," he says, low, firm, but respectful.

"I am aware," Thorne replies, his gaze fixed on my mouth. He leans in and places a tender kiss on my cherry lips. "But we all have other needs, other things we hunger for." Thorne's voice is low, decadent, and dangerous. "Stand still," he murmurs, stepping behind me, his cool lips ghosting my neck. He removes my underwear with patient, practised hands. A shiver runs over my exposed skin in the cool, stone chamber.

Thorne clicks his fingers, and Darius moves silently to the wall, lifting a plaited length of deep crimson rope from an iron hook. It gleams faintly in the candlelight, oiled and soft to the touch. Thorne takes the rope and with a single tug at each end of the braid, it unravels and the silky cord thumps softly to the stone floor, while on end remains in his slender grasp.

"Hands out, my darling," Thorne says, and when I obey, bending my arms at the elbows to present my hands, he takes my wrists in his long fingers, turning them over like he's inspecting precious artefacts. "Perfect."

They work in tandem without a single word. Darius binds my wrists together in front of me, the rope coiling with precise tension, neither too tight nor too loose. Thorne guides me across the chamber to a carved wooden frame standing near the bed—tall, arching, reminiscent of a cathedral doorway. An iron ring hangs from the top beam, and the moment I see it, my breath quickens.

"Lift her," Thorne orders.

Darius's hands span my waist and he hoists me effortlessly until Thorne hooks my bound wrists into the ring. I'm left standing on the tips of my toes, arms stretched high, my body fully displayed. The rope pulls just enough to remind me I'm not going anywhere.

Thorne steps back to admire the view, his silver hair catching the candlelight, his expression unreadable. I shiver under the combined weight of their gazes. Thorne closes the distance, his fingertips trailing from the inside of my elbow down to my ribs, to my hips, to the top of my thigh. "Exquisite," he murmurs, before delivering a sudden, sharp slap to my inner thigh that makes me gasp. "And mine to display."

He moves behind me while Darius kneels in front,

his mouth hot against my stomach, then moving lower. Thorne's hands skim over my shoulders, down my back, until they rest possessively at my hips.

"Do you feel that, my dear?" Thorne's voice is velvet-wrapped steel at my ear. "Two predators, one prey."

Darius's tongue is on me then, hot and unyielding, lapping in slow, deliberate strokes that make my knees weaken. Thorne tightens his grip to keep me upright, one hand sliding up to cup my breast, thumb teasing my nipple until it hardens under his touch.

When my moans grow louder, Thorne murmurs, "Stop." Darius obeys instantly, his mouth glistening, eyes locked on mine.

Thorne steps in front of me now, exchanging places. His mouth is cooler, more precise, and when he pushes two fingers inside me, the stretch is enough to make my head fall back between my raised arms.

"Hold her steady," he tells Darius.

Darius presses against my back, his chest a solid wall of heat against my spine, his hands bracketing my ribs as though I might come apart without him holding me together. The steady press of his body grounds me even as Thorne devours me, his mouth moving with a mastery that leaves no part of me untouched. Every flick of his tongue is deliberate, calculated to unravel me without letting me tumble fully over the edge.

I gasp, my breath catching in short, broken bursts. Darius's thumbs stroke slow circles over the swell of my breasts, teasing the edges of sensitivity until my nipples ache for his touch. His grip tightens each time I twist under Thorne's mouth, not harsh enough to hurt but firm enough to remind me I'm exactly where they want me.

Heat builds low in my belly, sharp and insistent, curling through me in dizzying waves. I feel Darius's strength supporting me—steady, controlled—while inside, I'm anything but. Every nerve ending seems to pulse in rhythm with Thorne's tongue, my thighs quivering under the strain of holding myself open for him. I'm trapped between them, caught in the delicious push and pull of restraint and release, and it's almost too much. Almost.

When Thorne rises, his lips wet, he says, "The bed."

The transition is swift—Darius lifts me from the frame, carrying me like I weigh nothing, laying me on the black silk sheets. My wrists are still bound, they're drawn above my head again and secured to the headboard with a quick knot from Thorne's skilled hands. They strip themselves as I lie there, bound and helpless, bodies moving with the unhurried confidence of men who know they own the night—and me.

"Open her," Thorne instructs.

Darius spreads my legs and kneels between them, the head of his cock already nudging at me. Thorne climbs onto the bed beside us, one hand in my hair, forcing me to meet his eyes.

"She will look at me while you take her," Thorne says. "Fuck her, now."

And Darius does, sinking into me with a deep, claiming thrust that has me arching off the bed. My bound hands tighten on the rope, my hips arching into him. Thorne strokes my jaw with his thumb, his gaze unreadable but electric.

They move in sync without speaking—Darius driving into me from below, Thorne kissing me with a bruising, claiming hunger. When I moan into his mouth, he pulls back just enough to say, "Not yet, little mortal."

He shifts lower, his mouth on my breasts, teeth grazing my nipple while Darius's thrusts grow sharper. Thorne's hand slides down my belly, finding my clit, circling with maddening control.

The two of them build me to the edge like master craftsmen, denying me until my whole body shakes with need.

Thorne's hand threads into my hair again, tipping my head back so he can press his cock to my lips. I take him in, the taste of him dark and electric, while Darius pounds into me from below.

I'm nothing but sensation—cool silk, rough heat, the sting of rope on my wrists, the steady rhythm of them moving with and against each other through me.

"Good girl," Thorne murmurs, the words a low vibration that makes my hips jerk. "Not yet. You don't come until I say."

A frustrated whimper escapes my mouth around Thorne's length, but Darius's voice cuts through my moans in a rasp of hunger.

"Do as he says," he groans, the sound raw enough to make me shiver.

Their voices mix—Thorne's dark praise, Darius's

ragged urging—until I can't tell where one ends and the other begins. Heat coils low in my belly, sharp and insistent, curling through me in dizzying waves, but I hold on, because they told me to.

"Now," Thorne says at last, and the command detonates something inside me. When my climax rips through me, it's violent, electric, my scream muffled around Thorne's cock. He spills in my mouth as Darius grinds deep inside me, flooding me with heat, the two of them wringing every last pulse from my body before finally easing me down into the sheets.

They untie me only to pull me between them, the aftermath as deliberate as the ritual—Darius's hands soothing over my thighs, Thorne's fingers combing slowly through my hair.

"Perfect," Thorne murmurs.

We stay tangled together in the cool hush of Thorne's chambers, my body still humming, my skin flushed and damp. Darius pulls the covers over us, one arm draped possessively around my waist. His thumb strokes idly along my hip, grounding me in a way that makes my chest ache.

Thorne lies on my other side, propped on one elbow, studying me like I'm a piece of art he's not yet decided whether to keep behind glass or on open display. He brushes a strand of hair from my face with surprising gentleness.

"I love to watch you breathe," he murmurs.

I smile, drawing slow air into my lungs, letting the weight of them—of this—anchor me. My wrists bear faint red marks from the rope, and Thorne's thumb ghosts over them, a quiet inspection, as though he's ensuring I'm still intact.

"You've done well, little mortal," he says at last, voice warm enough to steal the chill from the stone walls.

Darius presses a kiss to my temple. "Rest now. We'll watch over you."

I sink deeper into the cocoon of their bodies, the heady scent of sex and silk wrapping around me like a second skin.

It should feel dangerous. It should feel like surrender.

It does.

And I think—I'm not sure I ever want to be free.

They hold me between them, a mortal caught in the quiet aftershock of two predators' hunger. My pulse is slowing, my breath softening, but the ache they've left inside me feels endless.

My eyes grow heavy, and somewhere between waking and sleep, words from the mysterious book I've been reading slide through my mind like a whispered spell. *Desire is the story we dare not speak aloud*.

I close my eyes and smile in the dark.

Because I already know I'll let them write the next chapter in my blood.

# THE BOOKBINDER'S FAREWELL

You think you've escaped the bite.

But the story does not end with the closing of a book, my dear. Not when you've tasted what lurks in the shadows of Edinburgh, not when the touch of two possessive predators still burns in your blood.

There is one more chapter I have kept aside for you — a hidden page where pleasure and hunger entwine, and where the threads of your fate brush against another woman's... one who has also felt my hand in her story.

Step closer. Let me open it for you.

*You know you want to.*

# The Heat Doesn't Have to End Here

*Want more of Katrina, Thorne & Darius?*

Their hunger doesn't end here.

Download the free bonus epilogue and discover what happens when desire bleeds deeper, boundaries blur, and surrender tastes sweeter than sin.

Just one more bite…

You know you want it.

Download it here: https://BookHip.com/BHLQHHT

Sign up to my newsletter for exclusive bonus content—including epilogues you won't find anywhere else.

It's free, filthy, and just a little bit forbidden.

See you between the pages, gorgeous.

Lacey xox

Printed in Dunstable, United Kingdom